Dear Romance Reader,

Welcome to a world of breathtaking passion and never-ending romance.

Welcome to ***Precious Gem Romances.***

It is our pleasure to present *Precious Gem Romances,* a wonderful new line of romance books by some of America's best-loved authors. Let these thrilling historical and contemporary romances sweep you away to far-off times and places in stories that will dazzle your senses and melt your heart.

Sparkling with joy, laughter, and love, each *Precious Gem Romance* glows with all the passion and excitement you expect from the very best in romance. Offered at a great affordable price, these books are an irresistible value—and an essential addition to your romance collection. Tender love stories you will want to read again and again, *Precious Gem Romances* are books you will treasure forever.

Look for eight fabulous new *Precious Gem Romances* each month—available only at Wal★Mart.

Lynn Brown, Publisher

BACHELOR FOR SALE

JANET WELLINGTON

Zebra Books
Kensington Publishing Corp.
http://www.zebrabooks.com

To my mother, who taught me to love books, and to my dad, who always believed I would write one. And to my own hero, Jim, for patience and encouragement. This book is dedicated to you, the reader, with a reminder: Never underestimate the power of a dream.

ZEBRA BOOKS are published by

Kensington Publishing Corp.
850 Third Avenue
New York, NY 10022

First Printing: September, 1998
10 9 8 7 6 5 4 3 2 1

Printed in the United States of America

ONE

All I need is one cowboy for one night. No problem.

Lacey Murdock sat fidgeting in her car in the parking lot of the Rockin' Ranch country music bar. Early, as usual. She planned to use the extra time to calm her inevitable panic attack. She hated the feeling.

Her heart thundered and felt like it was ready to jump out of her chest. Her mouth was parched. Cottonmouth, she thought. With trembling fingers, she unfastened her seat belt. It suddenly felt much too confining, the shoulder belt threatening to choke the courage out of her.

I can do this. Forcing herself to breathe normally, she rolled down the window, immediately feeling relief as the balmy evening air cooled her damp skin.

She tilted the rearview mirror toward her and stared, taking a critical look at herself. *Hair okay.* Her thick, wavy dark hair fell to the middle of her back and shone with newly foiled auburn highlights. Setting gel kept its frizziness to a minimum, and she raked her fingers through her curls to lift them away from her hot neck.

Makeup okay. Lacey stared into her own eyes; the lilac eye shadow made her hazel eyes look green in the dim light. She blended the color with her little finger and checked for eyeliner smudges. Her makeup was much heavier than she was used to wearing, and the colors a shade brighter.

It's funny. I spend all day helping men and women enhance their looks, try new things, and I can't quite transfer the idea to me.

She readjusted her mirror, put her keys in her pocket, and slipped the skinny strap of her tiny new "going out" purse over her shoulder. She could already feel her stomach tighten with a bit of nausea. *Oh, great. No, I can do this. I just need to relax. Replace the oxygen, breathe deep five times.*

Lacey stayed in the car just long enough to take five measured breaths. The technique helped to calm her nerves and she used it at least once a day—whenever there was a new salon client, whenever the cash drawer wouldn't balance, whenever she had to counsel one of the other stylists.

At thirty-two she was finally making a decent living as the working manager of a mall-based hair salon in a suburb of San Diego. She'd survived a rough year, mostly by working hard, keeping herself distracted, and surrounding herself with happy people. People who really cared about her.

Tonight, though, her breathing exercise didn't seem to help much.

Outside the car, Lacey listened to the sound drifting from the windows of the Rockin' Ranch. She decided the music and conversation were definitely too loud—and too cheerful for her precarious mood.

The building that housed the bar looked like a barn, but with a wide porch that wrapped around the side and bordered the parking lot. Large rustic chairs lined the porch, ready and waiting for couples looking for a break from the heat of the dance floor. A few love seats were already filled with early arrivals, many of the women sitting on the laps of their dates.

As Lacey crossed the parking lot, she saw that most of the men sported the standard western look: cowboy hats, jeans, and boots. She couldn't help noticing that the majority of the jeans were tight, accentuating long legs and firm buns. It had been quite a while since she'd even allowed herself to look. Now she found herself actually examining the men. She hoped the dark concealed her blush.

She scanned the parking lot for Kandy's pink Jeep. No sign of it. Her friend was habitually late, and even though she was accustomed to it, she didn't relish the idea of entering the bar alone. She approached the porch with her head held high and her lips in a forced smile, silently reciting her new mantra: *I can do this, I can do this.*

A deep breath filled her lungs with the fragrance of night-blooming jasmine, and Lacey noticed a tall hedge of the flowers bordering the back of the parking lot. Better check there for Kandy's car, she thought, just in case.

As she followed the porch around the rear of the building, it widened into a large wooden deck, adjacent to the club's back door. A van was being unloaded nearby. As she scooted to a far corner of the deck to get out of the way, two men hurriedly carried a large amplifier up the steps and into the doorway, obviously on their way to the stage inside.

On the side of the van Lacey could just make out the words "Southern Comfort." The band was local, she knew, and quite popular. Kandy claimed they were the best country band around and she was a bit of a groupie, with a desperate crush on the lead singer.

Lacey instantly felt more comfortable in the darkness, alone on the deck. She leaned against the rail, laying her purse down. Recorded music drifted outside, and she began to move to the music, practicing a simple two-step, catching the beat, counting quietly out loud. "One, two, one . . . two. One, two, one . . . two."

She closed her eyes and lifted her arms, an imaginary partner in her arms. Her biggest fear was that she would end up stumbling awkwardly through her first dance. It had been a long time since she'd been on a dance floor, let alone dancing something as specific as a two-step, rudimentary as it was. Eyes still closed, she continued to move rhythmically, dancing blindly into the middle of the deck, counting softly to keep herself in step.

Jared Conrad ran long, calloused fingers through his hair in a feeble attempt to tame its wildness. Long days outside in the weather rendered an almost permanent windblown look. Subtle blond highlights blended with the gray that had become more prominent in his brown hair since he'd reached the deadly forties.

He sighed and shook his head. *That's as good as it gets.* He was already impatient for the evening to be over, even though he was grateful for the extra money the summer gig would provide. Even for short periods of time, he had trouble leaving his mountain and ranch behind. And Jamie.

He didn't particularly like being on stage, though playing bass in a country band was about as easy a job as he could imagine. He'd go insane if he didn't spend part of every day outside, though, and he knew he'd made the right choice in buying the llama ranch outside San Diego.

Being his own boss, setting his own hours, taking time to do the job right—each was important to him. Even though he had the pressure of being totally responsible for every little detail, he wouldn't have it any other way. He'd grown to prefer the solitude, the freedom. No one to interfere, no one trying to change things.

Jared locked up his truck and walked across the parking lot. His gaze stopped when he saw a woman who was carefully two-stepping to the soft music that filtered out the back door. It was evident he was about to interrupt a practice session and, although he knew he should make some noise in warning, he couldn't bring himself to disrupt the vision of her innocent dance.

Instead, he noiselessly positioned himself at the top of the stairs, crossed his arms, and watched. He openly stared, watching her full black skirt do a dance of its own, swirling around shapely legs. His gaze moved upward to her white cotton blouse, buttoned all the way to the neck, meticulously pressed. Perhaps because she was dressed so conservatively, he found himself wondering what her skin looked like. To his surprise, he found himself wondering what it might feel like.

Lacey had fallen into the natural rhythm of the music, her feet moving perfectly to the beat. *I can do this. I can do this.* She sighed with relief and opened her eyes.

"Oh!" She inhaled sharply and stumbled into Jared's arms.

Jared instinctively tightened his hold on her and felt his senses suddenly overload. In the briefest of moments, he was shocked to find his body responding to her, instantly aroused. In a timeless moment, he breathed her perfume, wanting to remember the scent of her. Reddish silky hair draped over one hand and he felt a hint of soft, warm flesh against the other. He realized his lips were automatically parting, ready to kiss her.

No. Just as quickly, Jared forced a return to reality and pulled away.

"I'd say you look like you just might be ready for a real partner." He adjusted his grasp, placing Lacey's right hand in his left, and lifted her other hand to rest on his shoulder.

"Now, most guys start out with the quick one, two part first." He looked down to the floorboards, seeing how tiny her feet looked in front of his own. "Ready? Watch our feet. One, two, one . . . two. One, two, one . . . two. That's it."

He looked up and watched as Lacey forced a weak smile. He knew she was embarrassed, but even so, she didn't miss a beat.

"By George, I think she's got it," he said in an exaggerated British accent.

Lacey returned her gaze to their feet, matching the movements, too mortified to look up for more than a few seconds at a time.

Ask for a cowboy and you get one. She stared at the blue-jeaned legs and the plain black boots. The boots looked comfortable and worn, but in a good way, she thought. She allowed her gaze to drift upward to the red cotton shirt, open at his neck.

At her eye level, a fine gold chain lay nestled in the dark chest hair at the open collar of his shirt. She could just make out a name charm hanging from the chain. It was one word: *Jamie.*

Lacey inhaled nervously, forcing her gaze to stay level with her dancing cowboy's chest. Part of her desperately wanted to run screaming to her car, to forget her entire plan. Surprisingly, another part of her felt grateful for the forced first dance. It lessened at least some of the pressure she felt.

Breathing deeply, she identified his scent as a mixture of apricot soap and a light cologne she recognized but couldn't quite place. In his confident grip, she finally relaxed enough to fall into a familiar, comfortable rhythm. Much too quickly, the music ended and she looked up into soft gray eyes.

A voice called from the doorway. "Jared, we have to start in ten minutes and Luke's mike isn't working. You wanna get your butt in here and bail us out?" The voice belonged to one of the men that had been carrying equipment to the stage.

Jared released his hold on her and stepped back. "Duty calls."

Lacey quickly turned to leave.

"You dance just fine," he added, his voice fading at the last word as though he had more to say.

"Thanks." She croaked out the word, then grasped the railing and hastily made her way down the steps. *Okay, Kandy, this is where you're supposed to show up and save me from embarrassing moments like this.*

In comparison, the crowded bar seemed much more appealing as she made her way around the corner to the front entrance.

A small line had formed at the entry way and Lacey waited behind a group of women wearing skin-tight jeans and skimpy tank tops. The entire group was being carded as they went inside and she wondered if this new generation had perfected fake IDs; they sure looked young enough to need them.

At the entry way, Lacey was stopped by an almost exact replica of the Marlboro Man.

"There's a three dollar cover charge tonight, ma'am, for the band." Hank parked his cigarette in the ashtray on the empty stool next to him.

Lacey stared. She had an extensive male clientele at the Shear Delight salon, but none was quite the head-turner as the man before her. His eyes were an almost too-bright turquoise blue—*contacts?* Long, feathered blond hair was expertly blown dry. His black hat was tipped back, revealing a clean-shaven face except for a soft, droopy mustache. *A cowboy with a baby face, dimples and all.*

Perhaps her task of finding a cowboy would be easier than she'd anticipated. He certainly looked the part.

She reached into her bag for a ten, automatically smiling back at the man, feeling a rush of warmth in her cheeks. Unexpectedly, she felt her nerves tense, suddenly not really wanting to be the object of his attention.

"First time here?"

Lacey nodded.

"Thought so." Hank took the money. He'd been handling the door for months to work off his unpaid bar tab *and* to cover the damage from the last brawl he'd been in. He didn't mind the job, and bragged that it was the best chance to check out the women as they arrived. It certainly was the best opportunity to see who was alone, and identify any new prospects.

"What's your name?"

Lacey's hand trembled slightly as she held it out for her change. Was his smile friendly, or just a tiny bit suggestive? With a shudder she quickly dismissed her thoughts as paranoid, deciding she was overreacting. The only men she was used to being around were in her work environment. There, she was in control.

Relax. She commanded herself to smile. She hadn't realized how out of practice she was in handling a simple social situation.

"What's your name?" he repeated.

"Lacey."

"Well, I'm Hank, Lacey. You better watch out for all those sharks on the dance floor, if you know what I mean."

Lacey's forehead wrinkled. "Pardon me?"

"I'll keep an eye on you—and you just let me know if I can be of service tonight."

Lacey marked his words as cordial. After all, she was a first-timer and it was perfectly appropriate for him to be friendly to her, or any other patron.

"Catch you later." Hank smiled, then turned his attention to the group of regulars waiting in the doorway behind her.

Lacey squared her shoulders and took a few steps into the noisy room, willing herself to stay calm. As the music paused briefly so the band could do a sound check, the sound of Kandy's infectious laughter grabbed Lacey's attention. Relieved, she smiled and hurried to her tardy friend.

She found her standing with a group of young women at the end of the bar.

"Hey, everybody, here's Lacey! Sorry we're late. I know, I know. You can set a watch by me always being a half hour late." Kandy laughed at herself, and then introduced her friends.

Lacey was so relieved to see her that she refrained from saying anything about her perpetual tardiness. With Kandy being a very young twenty-one, she had decided it was a fault that would probably lessen with time and maturity. Now with her there, she already felt more at ease in the club's environment. And for that, she was grateful.

Lacey assessed the group quickly. She guessed that they all had most likely been carded at the door, they looked so young to her. All were in faded jeans and either tank tops or crop tops, their makeup perfect and their hair in the latest style.

"So, Kandy, which one is the guy you like?" one of the women asked.

"The gorgeous one." As Kandy stared at the stage, her expression transformed into one of almost girlish worship. It was obvious she was infatuated *and* was thoroughly enjoying the experience. "Look for the best bod' and the cutest face."

Lacey joined the others in looking at the stage, admiring Kandy's honest appreciation of the object of her desire. She knew her type. Kandy liked men who were a little rough around the edges, but also big and cuddly as teddy bears. There were three men working on the center microphone and one fit the description perfectly.

"That's Luke, in the black hat." Kandy's voice almost oozed the words. She laughed and added, "And the thing is, he's a nice guy too."

Lacey found Kandy's hand and gave it a squeeze. "He's adorable. Have you given him a Complimentary Hair Cut card yet?" Over the last year she had helped Kandy build quite a salon clientele by encouraging her to utilize "the first one's free" technique.

"I plan to slip one into the pocket of those tight jeans tonight. I just can't wait to give him a really long, luxurious shampoo."

The group collapsed into girlish squeals and giggles at Kandy's remarks. Lacey smiled, feeling much more calm now that she was part of a group, albeit a rather young one.

"And don't you even think of trying to snag him for the bachelor auction, either. He's mine," Kandy whispered to Lacey. "You'll have to find some other handsome cowboy bachelor hunk to ask."

Lacey rolled her eyes, remembering their mission tonight was indeed to convince two men—cowboy-types, to be exact—to participate in the Most Eligible Bachelor charity auction at the mall. At least they hadn't been assigned to firemen or construction workers, she thought, picturing herself walking into the local fire station or onto a construction site to recruit a couple of single men. In comparison, cowboys should be easier, she thought.

Lacey groaned dramatically. "That's the absolute last time I send you to cover for me at a manager's meeting without specific instructions to sit on your hands and resist the temptation to volunteer for anything."

"Oh, stop worrying. All I promised we'd do was find a couple more eligible men for their silly auction. Besides, it'll do you good to get out and circulate again."

"You have ulterior motives, my friend." Lacey gently punched Kandy's upper arm. "Don't you?"

Kandy flashed a smile. "You, girlfriend, have been celibate much too long."

In response, the group of women surrounding them whooped in unison, echoing their approval.

Lacey covered her eyes with one hand. "Do you think everyone heard you or would you like to use the microphone?"

Kandy grinned. "Okay, I'll be good. Let's sit at the

bar. Is that okay with everyone? We're too late for the good tables. Next time I promise to be early so we can sit close to the dance floor." She led the group skillfully through the crowd to some open stools at the bar.

"And, because I was late, the first round's on me." Kandy pulled out her wallet, ready to treat her friends.

"Nothing for me, Kandy. I'll be right back." Lacey suddenly remembered her purse she'd left outside on the deck, and quickly excused herself to go outside to retrieve it.

Her purse was right where she'd left it, but was just being picked up by her dancing cowboy.

"Ah, I was just about to try to find you to . . . to return this to you." Jared stumbled over his words as he stared into Lacey's happy, smiling face. She was beautiful. He hadn't imagined it after all. Her hazel green eyes sparkled with recent laughter. As he stared openly into the face of the auburn-haired angel, he realized that for no logical reason he wanted like crazy to be around her.

"I was afraid it might fall off the rail into the parking lot." Lacey reached for her purse.

Jared let his fingers brush against hers as she took the purse, conscious that he'd positioned it to force the touch. He blinked in surprise and swallowed hard to bring himself back to normal. He definitely wasn't used to feeling this close to being out of control. *What's the matter with me?*

He desperately tried to think of something—anything—to say to her that would keep her there with him. He felt as ridiculously shy as he had in high school. He remembered those bashful days with a little pain, now, and quickly reminded himself he was an adult who indeed knew how to make conversation.

"So, do you come here often?" Jared groaned and laughed. "I can't believe I just said that. It's just that I haven't noticed you in here before."

Lacey grinned at his obvious openness and felt all the more comforted that she was not the only one who wasn't completely at ease. She examined his face because she couldn't decide exactly what it was that made him seem different. He could have easily blended into the crowd, with his western boots, jeans, and shirt. He wore no cowboy hat, for one thing, she decided, and his face looked a touch older than the majority of the people at the Rockin' Ranch. His hair was a chocolate brown, wavy, and cut in long layers that fell over his collar. She couldn't help mentally designing a new style for him. She also noticed more than a few fine strands of silver mixed in with the dark gold highlights.

Then she noticed the well-worn wedding ring on her dancing cowboy's left hand.

"It's my first time here tonight. I'm with some friends." Feeling suddenly cotton-mouthed, Lacey forced herself to take a deep breath before bravely adding, "And my name's Lacey—you're Jared, right?" At least he was safe to practice on, she thought.

Jared's brow furrowed, his expression questioning her use of his name.

"When they called you in to fix the microphone, didn't that man call you Jared?"

"A good dancer *and* observant. Lacey, you'll do fine tonight. I predict you'll be beating them off with a stick. In fact, just give me the high sign and I'll throw you a drumstick from the stage."

Lacey felt herself relax and begin to enjoy the banter. "So, are you a roadie or are you in the band?"

"To tell you the truth, I'm just filling in for part of the summer—substitute bass player. Glenn's wife just had a baby and he wanted to spend some time at home. So it worked out for both of us."

"Ah . . . substitute bass player *and* microphone mechanic." Lacey heard a drum roll from inside, then the crash of a cymbal. A cheer escaped from the crowd. The live music was about to start. "Well, I guess I better get back to my friends."

"And I better get back to work. Have fun tonight, Lacey." Jared nodded politely. He wanted more than anything to just grab her for the first dance and forget he had ever agreed to help out playing with Southern Comfort. Glenn needed a break, though, and he certainly could use the extra money, and the distraction.

But right now, for the first time in a long time, he was distracted by something else. By someone else.

Lacey smiled warmly and turned to go back to the bar. Her mood was improving by the minute. Her dancing cowboy was nice. Actually, he was more than nice, she corrected herself, but he was married. *Not a cowboy bachelor candidate.*

As they both paused briefly in the doorway, Jared reached to touch a curl of Lacey's long, dark hair. It was silky soft to his calloused fingertips. *Just like Jamie's.* Somehow he successfully fought the incredible urge to take a handful and bring it to his face. As Lacey continued into the bar, he quickly dropped his hand and walked onto the stage.

The rest of the band looked his way with interested expressions.

Lacey rejoined Kandy and her boisterous group gathered at the middle of the bar. All were giddily drinking shots of tequila, licking salt off their hands and biting limes. Lacey let out a long, deep sigh. She knew the night was going to be a challenge, but she was determined it would at least be fruitful.

And she wasn't leaving without procuring a cowboy for the auction.

TWO

Kandy eagerly pointed out the single men she knew in the room to Lacey. She included Hank, a.k.a. the Marlboro Man, in her long and descriptive list. Though she'd heard he was a flirt, she declared he was probably worth the trouble.

"He really is a cutie—*and* a good dancer. You should just ask him to dance. I'm telling you, he won't turn you down," Kandy said, staring at the band, her gaze now fixed on Luke. She bounced with the music, her upper body moving to the beat of the song.

Lacey groaned. "You're lucky I'm here even entertaining the thought of dancing with a stranger." Silently, she reminded herself that outside she had done just that, and she made a mental note to ask about her bass-playing, dancing cowboy later.

"Oh, Lacey, quit worrying about it." Kandy gave Lacey's knee a comforting squeeze. "Just chill; it'll be fine."

Lacey knew she needed to relax a little more and let down her guard. She even agreed to join the group in a shot of something very tasty that Kandy called a Watermelon. It reminded her of the watermelon-flavored hard candy she'd enjoyed in her childhood. Though she didn't care for the taste of alcohol, the liqueur was easy to drink because of its sweetness. It certainly took the edge off her nervousness, and she felt her anxiety ease a little.

As a popular line-dance song enticed Kandy and her friends to the dance floor, Lacey watched from the security of her barstool. Kandy danced quickly to the front, placing herself directly in view of Luke as he sang. The floor quickly filled with solo dancers who slipped into the familiar pattern of steps, while some couples ringed the outside in a slow two-step. Lacey studied the repetition of steps and smiled at Kandy's determination to hold Luke's attention.

Kandy was a good friend who knew her better than anyone. Most importantly, she'd been there for her during the last twelve months when she'd thought her whole world was falling apart. Though Kandy was immature in many ways, she had a level head and a solid foundation from growing up in a loving, supportive family.

Kandy had managed to help Lacey face the fact that even when everything seemed devastatingly horrible, life just went on anyway, and that ultimately everyone needed to look for a way out of their own unhappiness.

Kandy's solution had sounded so simple. Over egg rolls and chop suey at lunch one day, Kandy had convinced her that she had to give up the whole idea that life was supposed to be fair. In fact, she'd told her, life was basically unfair and she reiterated how each person was responsible for creating their own happiness.

Even Lacey's fortune cookie had agreed, affirming that "There is no way to happiness, happiness is the way."

From that moment on, Lacey's journey of healing had begun.

The previous year had been a roller coaster of ups and downs. Promoted to Salon Manager one month. Falling in love the next month. Then she'd been busy planning a wedding and picking out china.

Things had changed drastically in one dreadful day.

Lacey shuddered. Blake had appeared to be the perfect catch: handsome, charming, seemingly financially secure, and a single dad with a charming three-year-old son. She had fallen head over heels with him very quickly in their dating relationship. She had also fallen in love with his little boy.

Everything had seemed so wonderful, Lacey thought, remembering how ideal her world had seemed. Ideal until she'd called Blake's number in the middle of the day, intending to leave a romantic message on his answering machine.

She recalled how sick to her stomach she'd felt when a female voice answered the phone instead of his machine. Closing her eyes, she replayed the moment for the hundredth time. She had asked for him and was told he wasn't home. The voice sounded very young . . . and familiar. Somehow she had found the courage to ask who she was.

The voice had replied, "Heather. Who's this?"

Lacey had said nothing and quickly hung up the phone. Fighting the feeling of nausea that threatened to overwhelm her, with shaking fingers, she dialed Blake's work number.

After he'd listened to her accusations, he pleaded for a chance to explain and they'd met for dinner that evening. He confessed his affair with his secretary. She was pregnant and he would marry her. They planned to leave California, move to Texas to be closer to her family, who would help with the financial burden.

She'd left the restaurant in tears, her perfect life in shambles.

In the end, she'd discovered Heather was just part of a long list of lies. She had survived, but had been left with a hurt and a wariness that had kept her from dating over the last twelve months. She'd found she just wasn't that interested in men.

Sighing deeply, Lacey allowed the memories to fade. For the first time, the hurt was only a dull ache. The pain had lessened a little more each day over the last year. She had followed everyone's advice and kept as busy as possible, concentrating on her work, making the salon successful. She smiled, knowing that Kandy had been right about being responsible for her own happiness. She was okay now, and ready for her first step in returning to the world of the living.

Finally succumbing to Kandy's pleading, even before the bachelor assignment, Lacey had decided to at least start going out and having fun—start being social again. All the gals at the salon had encouraged her to be like the guys—avoid a serious relationship like the plague. They had persuaded her to learn to play the field a little and concentrate on just having a good time.

After weeks of prodding, Lacey decided to take a mature, logical approach to reentering the world of singles . . . she'd made a list of what she wanted. Firstly, no more single dads, she had resolved. She wouldn't take another chance on losing the love of another child if the relationship didn't last. She knew it would be too much for her fragile heart.

And she would look for someone younger, someone fun and adventurous.

She also decided to focus on physical traits that were the opposite of Blake's. She would look for tall and blond. Financially secure would help, she'd added. She ended the list with the requirement that her mystery man must respect and encourage her career, enjoy her independence. Her profession was extremely important to her, actually the most stable part of her life, nothing she would give up for anything . . . or anyone.

Lacey returned her attention to the jam-packed dance floor and smiled a small, secret smile, reciting to herself: *I can do this.*

"How 'bout a dance?" Hank had been watching Lacey. When he saw her friends go out to the dance floor, he also saw his opportunity.

Lacey looked into Hank's bright blue eyes and caught her breath. "Sure, but I'm just learning . . ."

Hank smiled and said, "Well, I'm teachin'—c'mon." He took Lacey's hand and led her to the edge of the dance floor, behind the line dancers. Expertly, he scooped her into his arms and began to two-step.

Lacey's eyes opened wide in concentration and she found herself naturally falling into the rhythm of the dance. She felt secure in Hank's hold and noticed how muscular his shoulder felt through his denim shirt. She was surprised how good it felt to be held tightly, being steered through the spinning couples. She slid her left hand down a bit onto his forearm, mimicking the position of the other dancers. Hank flashed a dimpled smile at her. He was even better looking at this close distance, she thought.

From the stage, Jared had observed Hank's approach and Lacey's delighted acceptance to join the dancers. *But mine was her very first dance.* He doubted she'd remember it that way, though. Luckily, the song was one he could play in his sleep because he found himself following Lacey and Hank's progress around the dance floor very carefully. Why did it have to be Hank, he thought. *Anyone but him.*

On stage, Jared's jaw tightened and the muscle there began to twitch. He consciously separated his clenched teeth and forced a smile. Three more songs remained in the first set and he needed to pay some attention to chords and key changes.

He'd watched Lacey leave the floor with Hank and shuddered at the thought of her in his arms. While they'd danced, he observed how Hank held her tightly, carefully guiding her around the perimeter of the dance floor, skillfully avoiding the line dancers.

Jared closed his eyes for an instant. He had no right even thinking about her. He was there to play a gig, nothing more. He should be oblivious to anyone—and everyone—in the club. *Then why am I acting like some young kid ready to fight for the girl?*

He certainly didn't need the angelic distraction of Lacey. Besides, she was not the type of woman he needed in his and Jamie's life right now—even if he was looking. She was too young, for one thing, probably a good ten or fifteen years younger than him.

With practiced discipline, Jared expelled from his mind the lingering thoughts of how soft Lacey had felt in his arms. It wouldn't be so easy to forget the flowery scent of her perfume that subtly mixed with her own unique feminine scent. The pleasurable assault on his senses had imprinted her fragrance in his subconscious memory. At least he could cherish the memory of their dance together. No harm in that.

The first set finally came to an end with another line-dance favorite. The band gave a hoot in chorus and Luke leaned into the mike, declaring the need to "pause for the cause." Guitars were quickly secured into their stands and the stage cleared.

Jared lagged behind the others, carefully placing his bass against the back wall, then flipped off his amplifier. Guardedly, he observed the path of each band member toward the bar.

He eyed the front door. He certainly needed some fresh air, and it wouldn't hurt his feelings any if he ran into Hank and Lacey.

THREE

"So, tell me about yourself, Lacey."

Lacey held Hank's gaze. "Oh, not much to tell, really," Though she suddenly found it difficult to take a deep breath, the alcohol in the drink Hank had bought her helped give her at least the temporary feeling of assurance and fortitude. "I'm just ready to start having fun again, I guess. And the Rockin' Ranch came highly recommended."

"Are you having fun yet?" Hank grinned, using her comment as an opportunity to move a little closer, just enough to place his thigh against hers. "I think you and me could have a whole lot of fun together." He tipped his glass against hers in a toast.

Drawing a long swallow from the straw, Lacey said nothing for a moment. *Why not?* "Perhaps we could," she replied.

"That's my girl." Hank reached his hand up to smooth an errant strand of hair off her cheek. He saw the color rise in her creamy skin, starting from her neck. He glanced downward and ogled the vee where her breasts met. *This one's going to be fun.*

Lacey closed her eyes at the touch of Hank's fingers on her cheek. She felt his fingers find their way behind her ear and then to the nape of her neck. Deep in her womanly depths she felt a tiny flicker of life. She welcomed the hint of an internal quiver as he pulled her closer, waiting a little anxiously for the feel of his lips on hers.

It was his mustache that she felt first, stiff, long hairs tickling her mouth. She waited. When his lips touched hers, they were dry, and the stale aroma of cigarettes was there. The alcohol helped mask it a little, she thought curiously. Almost with a feeling of being outside her body, observing the action, she responded shyly to his kiss, so foreign, so new. Breathless, she pulled away the moment she felt his tongue flick against her lips.

Hank kept his hand on her neck for a moment, then let his fingers drop to her shoulder and then to the middle of her upper arm. Deliberately he positioned his hand so that his thumb rubbed the curve of her breast as he let it fall down her arm to take her hand in his. Waiting another moment for a reaction, he smiled deeply. *Easier than takin' candy from a baby.*

Lacey caught her breath as she thought she felt Hank's touch her breast. Her head was swimming and beginning to throb a little. She pulled back from him, trying to find cooler, cleaner air to breathe, rubbing her temples as the throbbing escalated into a sharp jab of pain.

"Sorry. I guess that drink was a little too strong for me."

"Well, here, let me take care of the rest of that one." He poured the remains of her drink into his own empty glass. "And, unfortunately, dear lady, I have to return to the door. The late crowd is about to arrive. Catch you later, Lacey." Hank grinned and made his way back to his stool at the entrance. *Yep, this one's gonna be fun.*

Jared stood in the shadows, feeling like a Peeping Tom. *What am I doing?* The intensity of the emotion he'd felt as he'd watched Hank kiss Lacey was unanticipated. His mouth had filled with the sour taste of anger and he had trembled, fighting an almost overwhelming urge to rip Hank's head off. It made no sense. He knew nothing about the woman. Other than the fact that he was having crazy feelings about her, there was no real reason he should be upset that she had danced with some guy, kissed some guy. But the guy was a snake, he rationalized. And, no matter what, she deserved more.

At least Hank was gone now. He'd watched as he'd returned to his post at the door, already flirting with a fresh batch of preppie college girls dressed in designer jeans. *You just stay there, and stay away from her.*

Jared leaned against the rough wood wall, mystified. He'd never felt this protective about anyone but Jamie. His sweet, precious girl. His daughter meant everything to him, and he was not going to jeopardize their tranquility by getting involved with a woman, even one as lovely as Lacey.

When he opened his eyes again, the love seat was empty. Lacey was nowhere in sight. *Good. Now, just walk away from this.* Somehow, though, he knew it was going to be difficult. He felt frustrated with himself for his lack of logic, and for spying on this beautiful stranger. And she was a stranger. He knew nothing about her and he had no legitimate reason to even care about her.

Feeling a little flustered, Jared returned to the club. Inside, he flagged his favorite waitress and tipped an imaginary glass to his lips, his signal for a glass of ice water.

Gloria gave him her usual thumbs up and was back from the bar in a couple of minutes with an extra large glass. "What's with you? You look like you just lost a hundred bucks on a bad bet."

Jared rolled his eyes. "I'm fine, Gloria. Just a little cranky tonight, I guess."

Gloria's expression revealed she didn't believe a word coming out of his mouth. "Well, if you need a listening ear, you know I'm here." She handed him the glass and rested her tray on her hip, giving him a moment to reconsider.

The sound of a raucous high-pitched squeal made them both turn toward the bar. Luke was standing in the midst of a group of women, his arm around Kandy's waist. She was beaming with joy.

"Ah, Luke and his notorious jokes." Gloria shook her head. "I hope he knows how serious that blonde is about him. Kandy is in love, the silly thing."

Jared stared at the group, his gaze instantly fixed on Lacey. He noticed her blouse was still unbuttoned at the neck and, as she joined the others in the shared laughter, her long hair swung with each bob of her head.

Gloria observed Jared's stare, following it in Lacey's direction.

"Gloria, what do you know about the woman behind Kandy?"

"Why?"

"Gloria, just tell me." His vexation was evident.

"Well, she's single if that's what you mean," she teased.

Jared groaned. "Forget it. It's not important."

"Now, wait. Don't get your underwear in a bundle." She hadn't meant to irritate him. Jared was one of those sweet sensitive guys you didn't find all that often, great friend material. He was different than most of the other guys in the band; quiet and thoughtful, always making sure her car started at the end of the night; like the protective big brother she'd always wanted.

"C'mon, Jared, tell me. What's up?"

"Oh, I don't know. I met her outside, before we started playing. I'm just curious."

"Okay. First of all, she happens to be my hairdresser." Gloria patted her hair and tipped her head back in an exaggerated model pose. "And she works with Kandy. Actually she's Kandy's boss. And she's really nice."

"That's it?"

"Well, we talk about . . . everything . . . when she does my hair, but it's like attorney-client privilege, ya know?"

"Right."

Gloria saw a glimmer of disappointment in Jared's soft gray eyes. There was more to this story, she decided. "Okay, but only because I like you," she continued. "I know she's just getting over a bad time—her fiance ran out on her because he got his secretary pregnant. He took his kid and left town; pretty much broke her heart. Even from the start we all thought he was a rat."

And she's found another rat. "That it?"

"She's a great gal, Jared. She's young, talented, has a successful career, and finally ready to have a little fun, I hope."

Great. Another successful career woman. Just what I don't need. He'd certainly had more than enough of that scene. "Thanks, Gloria." Jared turned and stepped up on the stage. It was time to get back to work, and he was determined to just do his job, and keep his eyes off Hank—and definitely off Lacey.

Taking advantage of the noise generated from rinsing the shampoo from her elderly client's hair, Lacey whispered to Kandy, "Did you ask him?"

Kandy nodded. She folded and stacked several clean towels on the shelf above the three pink shampoo bowls at the back of the salon. Her eyes sparkled as she whispered dramatically, "He said yes, of course."

"Good. One cowboy down, one to go. What's he doing about missing a Saturday night at the club?" Lacey asked.

"Some of the other guys in the band want to come watch so they switched with the Wednesday night band for that Saturday. Cool, huh?"

"Anything else?"

"Details at lunch," Kandy whispered, "my ten o'clock is here."

Lacey grinned at her and wrapped a fluffy mauve towel around Mrs. Allen's head. She had a soft spot in her heart for her longtime shampoo-and-set customer. Mrs. Allen had followed her from beauty school to become one of her regular clients at the fancy mall salon. Seeing her every week provided an anchor to reality that had proved invaluable when times were erratic.

"Lacey, your hands are magic. I'd come in just for the shampoo even if I didn't need my hair done." Mrs. Allen sighed and rocked her head back and forth, stretching her neck.

"My pleasure, ma'am. Now come with me and let's make you gorgeous for that anniversary dinner."

Lacey's day continued, just as her week had, filled with regular customers and a fair number of walk-ins. She loved her job. She had a good crew. Over time, she had successfully weeded out all the egotistical hairdressers from the staff, leaving a team of hard-working, pleasant stylists.

Glancing at her watch, she decided to hide out in the back room and do a little reorganizing of supplies. No scheduled customers for the rest of the day meant she had the luxury of uninterrupted time to stock shelves and do some laundry.

After a few minutes of glorious quiet, the door opened. Kandy poked her head in the doorway. "Lacey, you better come out and take care of this one."

Lacey groaned as she watched Kandy disappear. Crossing her fingers, she hoped it wasn't yet another case of chlorine-green blond hair. She'd already had her share of color corrections, two this week alone—and the summer was only half over. Much too time consuming a task for the end of a long Saturday, she said to herself.

An attractive middle-aged woman waited in the lobby, a young girl almost hidden behind her. Tiny hands grasped and tugged at the woman's tangerine-colored gauze skirt. As Lacey approached them both, she heard the unmistakable sound of the youngster's muffled sobs. She watched as the woman crouched to the floor and scooped the little one into her arms, comforting her with soft, soothing sounds.

"It's going to be fine, sweetpea. Trust your Auntie Jo. It's not so bad, really."

"Hi, I'm Lacey." Dropping to her knees to put herself at the child's level, she hoped to get a better look at her new challenge.

"This is my niece, Jamaica. She's a little shy and we had a bit of an adventure today. We decided our hair was too long to start kindergarten next month." The woman made a scissors motion with her fingers, out of the view of the little girl.

Lacey nodded. "Let's have a look, sweetie. Okay?"

The little girl's strawberry blonde hair lay in long banana curls that reached to the middle of her back. When she straightened her head, she lifted it just enough for Lacey to see that she had created a dramatic asymmetrical look—the right side was at least six inches shorter than the left, and her bangs looked as though they'd been cut with pinking shears.

"Oh, honey, it's not so bad. I used to cut my own hair all the time. It was kind of fun, wasn't it?"

The little girl wiped her cheeks and looked up. Gray-green eyes filled with fresh tears. She nodded warily. "But it looks awful."

"Naw, it's just not done yet. But, you know what? I can finish it." Lacey held her hand out to the girl, who cautiously put her tiny hand in hers. Lacey flashed a smile. *What a little angel.* Already she could envision how she would cut the little girl's hair. A shorter style would make her look older, she thought, but with the natural curl that was there, she knew she could maintain the cherubic appeal.

"Kandy, will you find my magic scissors, please, and we'll meet you over at my chair."

The little girl's eyes widened and she looked at her aunt, waiting for permission.

"Go on, now, this nice lady will take care of you. I'll be right here. Don't you worry." Breathing a loud sigh, the woman sank into one of the plush chairs in the lobby, visibly relieved that someone else was in control.

Lacey loved cutting children's hair. The feel was different; silky, immature hair that had to be cut carefully, *with* the curl, if there was any. On the way to her station she grabbed a booster seat.

The little girl climbed into Lacey's hydraulic chair, allowing the styling cape to be fastened around her neck. "It's pretty in here. Pink's my favorite color."

"I'm glad you like it. I like pink too." Lacey had chosen a glittery hot pink cape in hopes of distracting her and, so far, it seemed to be working. "Now, where are those magic scissors." She looked around the salon and nodded to Kandy, who ceremoniously brought her a midnight blue velvet pouch.

Gently, she misted the little girl's hair with water and combed out the tangles. With her expensive, tiny European gold shears in hand, Lacey began to shorten and layer the hair, retaining a little length in the back and cutting the front and sides so the strawberry blonde curls framed her face. She kept the chair facing the mirror so the little girl could watch, and talked soothingly throughout the process. From time to time she glanced at the woman waiting in the lobby, who smiled and nodded her blessing.

Lacey asked innocuous questions, weaving through conversations about Sesame Street, My Little Pony, favorite animals, and Disney videos. She could feel the little girl relax as she worked, and soon her gray-green eyes brightened and her smiles came more frequently. When she was finished, she handed the little girl a mirror, twirling her in the chair to show her how to look at the back of her head.

Her hair had dried while Lacey worked and she fluffed the now-layered curls into place. The hair was soft as silk in her fingers, luminous with reddish blonde highlights that shimmered under the salon lights.

As a last touch, Lacey opened the cupboard at her station to retrieve a final surprise. "And here is your fairy princess halo." She watched the little girl's expression in the mirror as she placed a circle of glittery metallic pink garland on her head, complete with iridescent streamers of star garland that fell to the spot where the strawberry blonde curls had once been.

"Oh, I look . . . beautiful." The little girl whispered the words, awestruck at the final results.

"Yes, you do, Princess Jamaica. Let's go show your auntie."

All smiles now, the little girl walked gingerly to the lobby, not wanting to upset the sparkling wreath she wore.

The woman's face glowed with relief and delight as she watched her niece walk carefully toward her. "Lacey, you are a magician. Look at my little princess. Your daddy is going to love it, honey."

Lacey shared the woman's relief. Another crisis solved. If only they were all this easy.

* * *

"Daddy, I'm a princess! She said so!"

The sun glared painfully in Jared's eyes as he looked up from brushing off his earth-covered boots. All he could make out was a bouncing shape running toward him from his sister's car.

"Look, Daddy, look!"

Jared watched as his daughter twirled and danced for his benefit, a private recital of innocent joy. He also watched as his sister Jo approached, giving him her best "don't you dare say a word" glare.

"Jamaica," she pleaded, "stop spinning and show your daddy your new hairstyle."

Jared rubbed his stubbled chin. Gone were his baby's long golden locks, replaced by bouncy curls and topped by something pink and glittery. After checking for clues from his sister's expression, he took the easy way out. "Well, let me see, Jamie. Tell me all about it."

Relieved at her brother's neutral response, Jo sighed. "Thanks for letting me have her today, Jared. We had . . . fun." She winked and waved a quick goodbye. "See ya."

"Daddy, she was a magician, kind of. Well at least she made my hair so pretty and she gave me my fairy princess hat and everything."

Jared's heart skipped a beat as he listened to the happy tumble of words come out of his daughter's little mouth. "Stand still for a minute and let me have a look. My, you look old enough for first grade, let alone kindergarten."

Jamie beamed at her father's approval.

"Now come here and give me a hello hug, you rascal."

"Oooh, Daddy. You need a shower." Jamie giggled and they began a favorite game of tag.

"Okay, okay. You win." Jared fell ceremoniously to the ground, flat on his back. Jamie took the opportunity to triumphantly plop squarely on his stomach.

"You really like it, right?" Jamie asked in a small voice, still looking for reassurance.

"It's perfect. You look beautiful."

"Thanks, Daddy. That's what the lacey-lady said too. She said it was because of the magic scissors and Auntie Jo said I was Princess Jamaica."

Jared's attention froze on his daughter's words. "Where did you have your hair done, Jamie?"

"At the mall. At the really pretty pink place . . . where the lacey-lady is."

"Ah, and I bet it was scary, huh?"

Jamie giggled. "Oh, Daddy. It was fun. Do you like my princess hat?"

Jared pushed himself up on his elbows to better look into his daughter's sparkling gray-green eyes. She looked less and less like her mother, he thought, and he was glad. Marsha had hoped Jamie's hair would stay white blonde, more like the bleached style she had started wearing the year she'd taken a job as a flight attendant. Jamie had been barely two then, and Jared had gladly kept his little girl with him as he worked on the ranch. He had fashioned a safe play area using bales of hay, and had relished watching her discover the wonder of nature, growing healthy and strong in the fresh mountain air.

As he gazed at his beautiful, jubilant little girl, he found very few traces of her mother. With a certain regret, he had finally realized that he was glad Marsha had left. After far too many fights in their short marriage, she had declared her career more important.

He never felt she had bonded with Jamie anyway, balking at breast feeding and insisting on a nanny the moment she'd come home from the hospital.

"Daaaaa-dy."

"Yes, sweetpea, I like your princess hat. Now, tell me about the lacey-lady."

"She's the boss of the hair place. Auntie Jo said she was. And she fixed my hair. She's pretty, Daddy. Her hair is long and dark like yours . . . but kind of shiny."

Sounds like the same Lacey to me. "And she sure cut your hair nice, sweetie. Let's go celebrate, okay? Ice cream after dinner . . ."

"Hot fudge sundae?"

"Deal."

"Can I wear my princess hat?"

"Yes, your highness, now get off me so I can fix our dinner so we can go get dessert."

Jamie squealed as he tickled her just enough to move her off his stomach. "Go play for half an hour and I'll call you to dinner. And stay out of the llama pens." Jared watched his daughter scamper toward the barn, pleased she had the kind of imagination that kept her forever discovering new adventures on the ranch. He hoped it would be enough to carry them both through the difficult growing-up years to come.

Being a single parent seemed luxurious now, when his daughter was young and thought he walked on water, but he knew things would get complicated soon enough. She'd discover boys and dating and . . . Jared shuddered. Enjoy today, he commanded himself. He hoped he would have the strength to survive her teenage years.

Silently he thanked his sister. She'd always been there to support him, assuring him he was a good father, consoling him when he feared he was making mistakes. He would rely on her for more and more, he knew, as Jamie matured.

In the kitchen of the snug three-bedroom dome home, Jared nuked a couple of vegetarian burritos and grabbed a fresh bag of tortilla chips and the mild salsa that Jamie liked. Not the best supper in the world, he thought, but it would get them down off the mountain and to the ice cream shop a little sooner. Then back in time to greet the babysitter.

If they stayed on track, he'd have just enough time to get to the Rockin' Ranch by nine. He couldn't help wondering if Jamie's "lacey-lady" would be there.

FOUR

"Man, oh, man, you have *got* to see the latest filly that is about to enter my stable."

Jared cringed at the sound of Hank's cocky drawl, instantly convinced he was referring to Lacey. He remained in the shadows at the foot of the back porch stairs, his guitar case in one hand, shamelessly eavesdropping as Hank bragged to one of his chums.

"So, what's she like?" A loud beer belch followed the man's question, inducing an even louder belch from Hank in return.

"She's not much of a dresser but she's got a set of jugs on her that can make a man forget what she's wearing." Hank chuckled nastily.

Jared's jaws clenched in response, his free hand in

a tight fist. A cold knot formed in his stomach as he ordered himself to be silent.

"You sure she'll show?"

"Oh, yeah. She promised me she'd be here tonight. Said she had somethin' to ask me. Besides, she's one of those virtuous types, all trusting and innocent. Should be a piece of cake to get her to come home with good ol' Hank."

The two men snickered and Jared clenched his mouth tighter, his back molars grinding. *You don't deserve to be in the same room with her, let alone touch her.*

"You wanna put some money where your mouth is?" the man asked, emphasizing his point with another belch.

"Sure. Twenty bucks says she's fixin' me breakfast tomorrow morning."

"You're on."

Jared listened to the sound of heavy footsteps as the two men walked toward the door. Just before they reached the doorway they gave their beer bottles a toss. The sound of shattering glass sent them into hysterics as Hank shouted "two points" before they stepped inside.

Well, at least I know where all the broken glass comes from. Jared tried to calm his ragged breath. Intense, unexpected anger threatened his control.

He closed his eyes. *It's none of my business. She's a big girl. She can take care of herself.*

When his bloodpressure finally returned to near normal, Jared walked into the club. Maybe she wouldn't be there. Maybe she wouldn't come.

"Is that what you're wearing?" Kandy gave Lacey a disapproving look as she stood steadfast in the doorway of her apartment. Hands on her hips, she pursed her lips and shook her head.

"What's wrong?" Lacey asked.

"Well, first of all, you wore that skirt *last* Saturday. And second, you will absolutely roast if you try to get through the night with long sleeves."

The same thought had crossed Lacey's mind as she had raced from her air-conditioned car to Kandy's air-conditioned apartment. The evening air was still sweltering with an early August heat wave and it didn't look like things were going to cool down anytime soon.

"Come with me right now and we'll find something cooler you can borrow for tonight."

Lacey obediently followed Kandy to her bedroom and into an enormous walk-in closet. No wonder she never saw Kandy in the same thing twice in a month. The contents of the huge closet were meticulously organized and color coordinated, with one whole wall of shelves that betrayed Kandy's passion for shoes.

"I can't believe this. How many shoes do you have?"

"Oh, maybe a hundred or so. Call me Imelda Marcos and you wear rags tonight," she threatened.

Lacey laughed. The rainbow array of colors was staggering and she walked toward a section of pastels, her fingers lightly touching the fabric of several garments. "It looks like a department store in here."

"Hush. Everyone should develop a hobby—mine just happens to be shopping."

"No wonder you always look great. I've always admired how you put separates together, and accessorize. You really have a wonderful fashion sense. I think I could use some lessons."

Kandy glowed from the compliment. "Anytime, boss, anytime. Now, let's see what we have for the shy, workaholic salon manager in search of a cowboy bachelor . . ."

Lacey watched in awe as Kandy grabbed dresses, held them up to her chin, quickly rejecting them or setting them aside to consider.

"This is my final recommendation, madame."

Lacey held the dress in front of her and looked in the oversized, full-length mirror. Kandy had picked out a dusty peach gauze sun dress with a scooped neck and full skirt. The material was whisper soft and felt cool and light to her fingers.

"We'll add this scarf as a belt, throw a quick french braid in your hair and we're off," Kandy announced.

"I love this dress. And the tags are still on it. Why haven't you ever worn it?"

"I don't know. It just didn't appeal to me once I got it home. I knew it would come in handy some day. If you like it, you can have it."

"Kandy, I couldn't . . ."

"Hurry up and get changed. Go on . . . a new dress always brings good luck. I'll pour us a couple of glasses of iced tea while you dress."

Lacey removed her black skirt and long-sleeved flowered blouse and then pulled the dress over her head. She frowned at her reflection. The neckline was cut a little too low for her taste. She wasn't used to showing so much skin. She looked again, smoothing the skirt and knotting the brightly colored scarf at her waist. Satisfied, she did a little twirl in the middle of the closet, watching her reflection in the mirror. It was a great dress for dancing.

Maybe it was the dress, maybe it was just time, but suddenly she felt a return of the old confidence she'd felt when she'd discovered her talent for doing hair.

She drew her shoulders back and lifted her chin. *Look out cowboys, here I come.*

As she climbed out of Kandy's jeep, Lacey was glad she had taken Kandy's advice. She would have been miserable in anything but the lightweight dress she was wearing.

"Are you sure you don't mind me going in early to sit with Luke?"

Lacey looked at her watch. "It's only fifteen minutes before they start letting people in. I'll just hang out here on the back porch. You go have fun. I'll see you inside."

She watched Kandy hurry to a side door where Luke was gesturing her to come in. They made such a cute couple, Lacey thought. Luke had come in for his free haircut during the week and Kandy had outdone herself. She had even talked him into getting a partial perm to give the top of his hair more body.

Luke had happily fallen under Kandy's spell. He'd seemed genuinely pleased to be asked to participate in the bachelor auction. Kandy was in seventh heaven and nearly impossible to be around all week.

Lacey settled in a corner on the back porch, resting her elbows on the rail. She closed her eyes and breathed the musky air, a blend of jasmine and something else. Roses, perhaps, she thought.

In her mind she rehearsed her invitation for Hank to take part in the bachelor auction, hoping for an affirmative answer so her task would end. Though she had danced with other men, he was certainly the best-looking, and he was the type of man she was sure the committee had in mind.

The sound of footsteps grabbed Lacey's attention

and her eyes flew open. She turned and immediately recognized her mysterious dancing cowboy walking toward her.

"Well, Jared, we meet again."

"Evenin' Lacey. Hot enough for ya?"

She grinned at his feigned sarcasm, pleased to see him. She'd enjoyed their banter the week before and a part of her hoped she might run into him again. He seemed like a nice guy. Not forward—safe, in fact. "Just hot enough, thanks."

"I wondered if you'd be here tonight," he continued, trying to control his mixed emotions. During his thirty-minute drive to the club he had been engulfed with thoughts that had turned into an overwhelming desire for an evening *without* the vision of Lacey in Hank's arms on the dance floor. But here she was.

Almost everything about her seemed different. She was more at ease, he decided. Not so conservatively dressed, either, he noticed. His gaze dropped to take in her dress, bare neck, and slim waist wrapped in a multicolored scarf. Her gauzy dress was a shade of orange he knew must have some sort of delicate name. The secrets of women's fashions totally eluded him.

All he knew was how breathtakingly beautiful Lacey looked. He noticed the absence of her hair on her shoulders and was disappointed that it was secured away from her face. He was surprised to discover his fingers craved to touch her silky tresses once more.

Lacey forced a smile as her mind clouded. *Was he coming on to her?* He's married, she reminded herself.

Cocking his head to the music drifting out the back door, Jared boldly continued. "To be honest, this is one of my favorite songs . . . being in the band, I don't get much chance to dance," he said. "Would you care to?"

Lacey furrowed her brow. *Okay, be calm. Think of something to say.*

She glanced at the hand Jared offered, then blinked hard. Where there once was a wedding ring, now only a pale ring of untanned skin existed.

Somehow, her feet took her forward and she extended her hand to take his. Within seconds they fell into the natural rhythm of the music, dancing a traditional slow dance.

Lacey breathed deeply. His scent added to the blend of night fragrances. He smelled clean. Again she noticed a hint of apricot soap and a light cologne. Her fingers lay comfortably on his shoulder and, as he drew her closer, she allowed them to cradle his neck. Her gaze fell on the golden charm she'd noticed the week before. *Okay, so, who is Jamie?*

As the words of the song declared that "true love waits," she found that her fingers had somehow gotten lost in the hair at the back of Jared's head. Soft, silky hair. Still damp at the nape from a recent shower.

Neither said a word as the music ended and they reluctantly stepped apart, but not until Jared had placed a gentle kiss on her cheek.

Jared broke the silence. "Thanks. I've always loved that Buddy Holly song and I can't remember ever having the chance to dance to it."

Lacey gazed at him, feeling confused and curious. *So, Mr. Dancing Cowboy, what happened to your wedding ring?*

As though her thoughts had been said aloud, Jared touched the charm and said, "By the way, just in case you wondered, Jamie's my daughter."

A strange mixture of relief and disappointment escaped from Lacey in a quick outgoing breath. He had a *daughter.*

"And I'm not . . . I'm a . . . single dad." The words tumbled out and he stared at her, seemingly waiting for a response.

Lacey met his gaze. "Anything else?" She tried to keep her tone light, a little distant. "You're really a Secret Agent? Bass player imposter?"

Jared visibly relaxed at her joking manner.

"I just got to thinking that I may have given you the wrong impression last week and just wanted to clear things up."

"No problem." She tried to keep her voice cool and aloof.

"Thanks again for the dance. I better get inside and set up."

Lacey's gaze followed Jared as he hurried into the club. *Too bad I'm not in the market for a single dad, Mr. Dancing Cowboy.*

She sighed. No single dads. Not after everything Blake had put her through. She mentally reviewed her list. No kids. A man her age or younger—though Jared's graying temples were awfully attractive, she thought. And no starving musicians either. *You promised to stick to your list.* Her own scolding thoughts rattled in her head as she pivoted on her sandaled heel and made her way to the club's entrance. There, with any luck, she thought, Hank would be waiting.

Jared almost tripped as he stepped onto the stage, his guitar case banging painfully against his shin. He winced and softly cursed, grateful that the rest of the band was sitting at the bar.

Lacey had come after all. *And I still got the first dance.* His attraction to her still pooled in his groin, he turned his back to the dance floor, hoping he could pull himself together before anyone noticed.

She looked different, much prettier than he had allowed his memory to capture. And that dress . . . bare armed, low-necked, silky soft, sexy, swirling skirt. She was definitely more beautiful than he'd remembered. *And her hair was different.* Sides pulled back from her face in a braid, with just the back hair hanging. He'd managed to slip his hand under it while they danced so he could hold her closer. Soft, silky angel hair.

Get a grip, Jared. He was irritated with himself. Frustrated. Turned on. That was the worst part. He had not expected his body to be so out of control. He shook his head. She's not your business, he reminded himself.

As he checked his amplifier and each cord for good connections, he glanced at the front door. Lacey was talking with Hank, their heads close together. He saw that Hank stayed seated, giving him an obvious opportunity to look down the front of Lacey's dress.

Snake. What could she possibly see in that guy? Jared continued to stare at what looked like a serious conversation.

Jared watched as Hank stood up, removed his hat with a sweeping gesture, and said loud enough for everyone in the room to hear, "I'd be honored, ma'am."

What was that all about?

Gloria's tapping foot interrupted his thoughts as she stood at the end of the stage with a tall glass of ice water. "Hey, hon', what's up?"

Jared tore his gaze from the doorway. "Gloria, do you have any idea what your hairdresser could possibly see in Hank Erickson?"

Gloria hesitated a moment. "By the tone of your voice, I'd say you really have something else on your mind."

Jared groaned. "What I don't need is for you to analyze me every time I ask you a question."

"Still cranky, I see. What's goin' on with you? I've never seen you this perturbed before."

"Did you hear what they were talking about at the door just now?"

"Who?"

"Hank and . . . Lacey."

"Now, why would you care a hoot what they were discussing?"

Jared frowned at the question. *Exactly. Why do I care?*

Gloria handed him the glass of water. "Drink this and cool down, Mister Nosey, and I'll tell you."

Jared drained the glass and handed it back.

"Better?"

"Better."

"Okay. The mall where Lacey's salon is has a charity event each year. This year it's a Dream Date Bachelor Auction. They've got every profession represented—"

"And that has exactly *what* to do with Hank?"

"Like I was saying," she continued, "there will be good looking and eligible firemen, construction workers, executives, policemen—get it?"

Jared nodded. "Sounds like The Village People to me."

Gloria gave him her best you-better-hush-and-let-me-finish scowl. "And Lacey and Kandy had to come up with two cowboys. Kandy asked Luke, and Lacey asked Hank. Happy now?"

Jared's mouth fell. "She asked Hank?"

"What is your problem, sugar? Are you sayin' you have an interest in my hairdresser?" she teased.

Jared glared his response.

"Well, if you do, you'd better think about doin' somethin' about it other than being cranky all night." With a grin, Gloria twirled and returned her attention to the tables filling up with the first customers of the night.

Jared's glance flitted from Gloria to see where Lacey was sitting. *Maybe I will.*

FIVE

Jared's jaw ached from clenching his teeth, a by-product of his inability to keep his gaze off Lacey all evening. A couple times she caught his stare and flashed him a smile. She sat at a table close to the dance floor with Kandy and the same group of women as the week before.

Unless she was dancing with Hank, that is.

Eleven. Eleven times she was in his arms. When she tried to dance with anyone else, Hank quickly cut in. Jared lost his place during one of the band's easiest tunes when he saw Hank's hand drift slowly downward until his fingers touched the curve of Lacey's bottom.

His heart soared as she pushed Hank away slightly, just enough to force him to reposition his hand. *Good girl.*

Lacey disappeared with Hank only once during the band's breaks. During the rest, Jared positioned himself as close to her table as he could, hoping to overhear conversation. No luck. The club was too rowdy for that. He spent the entire evening on pins and needles. Waiting.

After the last song, he shook his head in confusion. *Waiting for what?* Like Gloria said, he needed to either do something or forget it.

He watched as Lacey allowed a very inebriated Hank to lead her outside.

It was now or never, he thought. As soon as the equipment was stowed, he would find her . . . and warn her, whether she wanted to hear it or not.

Jared was on stage, packing his bass and meticulously winding cords when Lacey walked up.

"The music was good tonight." She spoke slowly and deliberately, anxious to keep her voice steady, especially after what had just happened outside. Her cheeks were flushed and hot, her wrists beginning to ache.

"Thanks. I enjoyed watching you dance to it."

She heard an unfamiliar caustic edge in his voice. Taking a deep breath, she continued. "Are you in a position to rescue a damsel in distress?"

Though his voice sounded neutral, Jared's face betrayed his concern. "What's wrong? Flat tire? I'm sure Hank would be happy to—"

"I'm not really interested in Hank's help right now," she interrupted. She bit her lip, the only way to keep it from quivering. *Please just say yes. Don't ask what happened.*

Jared's eyes narrowed. He turned and finished stowing some equipment and picked up his guitar case.

In a painful flash, the lights came on in the club, accompanied by a loud shout of "Last call. Drink 'em up or lose 'em." Lacey's hands flew up to shade her eyes from the sudden glare.

When her eyes adjusted she saw Jared's gaze locked on her wrists. Hot, red rings were quickly turning into bruises. Tears welled in her eyes, blurring her vision.

"I . . . I need a ride home. . . . I could call a cab, I guess, it's just that I thought you might be able to help me out and . . ." The words tumbled out in one breath. *Please say yes. Please say yes.*

"I thought you came with Kandy."

"She left already. She thought I was leaving with—"

"Hank." Jared finished her sentence, bridled anger in his voice.

Lacey blinked in surprise.

"Glad to be of assistance," his voice softer now. "I'll meet you outside in five minutes, okay?"

Lacey sucked in her breath, welcome relief washing through her.

"I'll say my goodbyes and settle with the band. You can meet me by my truck out back."

Lacey casually dabbed the corner of her eye, catching a tear before it escaped. She forced a smile and nodded. "Great."

Jared watched as she walked out the back door. *Damsel in distress? What was that all about? And something tells me that Hank had something to do with those bruises on your wrists.* With his mouth set in a determined line, he collected his pay and strode out the side door to the parking lot, determined to hear the whole story.

Wordlessly Jared unlocked the passenger door, slid his guitar behind the bench seat and offered her his hand. He caught her gaze for only an instant. She seemed embarrassed, but allowed him to help her into the truck.

He climbed behind the wheel. "So, where to?"

She answered him in a quiet voice, asking if he knew her street. He stared at her hands, now lying motionless in her lap. Even in the dim light of the parking lot, he could see the red edges of the bruises turning black and blue.

He caught her gaze again as he backed the truck out. She quickly looked away.

Jared waited for several minutes before he cleared his throat and asked, "What happened with Hank, Lacey?"

At a stoplight, he turned and looked at her. The dashboard lights bathed her face in a soft yellow glow. She turned her face to the window, away from his scrutiny.

"I'm fine, really," she began. "I didn't mean to lead him on . . ."

Jared winced at the confessional sound in her voice. "Let me tell you a little something about Hank. He's not what he seems."

Lacey turned her face in his direction, then tipped her head back a little and smiled. Her eyes shimmered with unshed tears.

Jared returned her smile. *She was a tough one.* "How are your wrists?" He returned his eyes to the road.

"Sore, but I'll ice them when I get home."

"I should have warned you about him earlier," Jared mumbled.

"I'm a big girl."

Jared flinched at the offended tone in her voice. "I only meant that he's very good at taking advantage of innocents—"

"Turn here," she interrupted. "You can let me off

at the sidewalk." She indicated a small house snuggled between two apartment buildings.

"Look, I didn't mean to insult you, it's just that Hank had it in his head that you were going to be his latest conquest and—"

"And poor little me certainly wouldn't be able to handle him," she finished, sarcasm dripping from her voice.

Jared groaned. What happened? He rescues her and she's mad. *Women.*

The truck stopped with a jerk. Lacey sighed. "I'm sorry. It's been a long night and I just need it to end."

Jared opened his door, intending to walk Lacey to her front door.

"I'm fine," she assured him, quickly opening the car door and slamming it shut.

With one foot on the pavement, Jared stopped, his mouth gaping in disbelief. *What an ingrate.* Maybe he was wrong about her.

As soon as he saw her go safely inside, Jared drove away, his head shaking in wonder.

Her back against the door, Lacey finally allowed a tear to escape from her tightly closed eyes. Hank *was* a jerk, but *she* was the idiot.

She wiped the tear from her cheek. Hank didn't deserve her tears, she thought, then shuddered as she looked at her wrists.

Refusing his invitation to go home with him, she naively thought he would accept a polite "no thanks." When he tried to kiss her and she turned away, her wrists were suddenly behind her back in a painful vice grip. Immobilized.

The sour smell of his breath was nauseating, but

adrenalin kicked in enough for her to threaten "the family jewels" if he didn't let go. With an unpleasant belch, he released her and mumbled "bitch" as she stormed away, her emotions a sickening mixture of humiliation and fury.

Throbbing pain reminded her of the need to ice her bruised wrists, proof of her naivete. She shook her head in frustration, running cold water on her hands at the kitchen sink.

Looks are deceiving, she reminded herself. Or maybe he just had too much to drink. *Or maybe I just don't know how to pick men.*

The sound of the phone disturbed her thoughts and sent her heart racing. Who would call at this hour? Wiping her hands on a towel, Lacey snatched the phone from the wall before its second ring.

"What are you doing home? I was expecting the machine."

Relieved to hear Kandy's voice and not a stranger telling her someone had died, Lacey laughed. "Hello to you, too."

"What are you doing there? I left right after the last set to meet Luke for coffee. He said you and Hank were—"

"Why the hell is everyone assuming Hank and I are a . . . a . . . couple?" She spat out the description. "Is there some sort of rule about dancing with someone and all of a sudden you're an item?"

"What's wrong? Are you all right?"

Lacey counted to five. Why was she so angry? Kandy had nothing to do with the whole situation. *Men.*

"Do you want me to come over?" Kandy asked.

"I'm just tired. Hank was so sure I was going home with him, and Jared thinks I'm an innocent—"

"Jared? What's he got to do with anything? Talk to me . . ."

Lacey shouldered the phone so she could take a bag of peas from the freezer. She wrapped it in a paper towel and put it on the table, then sat down and rested her throbbing wrists on it.

"Talk to me," Kandy repeated softly.

"I asked Hank to be in the auction, as planned. He said yes, as long as I promised to bid on him and win."

"I had to promise Luke the same thing," Kandy said.

"I think he just had way too much to drink tonight. Anyway, he assumed he was taking me home with him and he wouldn't take no for an answer."

"What do you mean?"

"You know that self-defense class we took at the mall? Well I almost got the opportunity to try out a groin kick."

"Geez, Lacey, did he hurt you or—"

"I'm fine, really. Just mad and upset. He seemed . . . okay, you know?"

"What about the auction?"

"He knows the rehearsal is Thursday night. I guess I'll have to wait and see if he shows." Lacey could hear a muffled sound in the background as though Kandy had put her hand over the receiver. "Kandy?"

"I'm here. Luke's here too," she whispered. "I feel so bad about deserting you—how did you get home?"

"Jared."

"Ahhhhh. And . . . ?"

"And he got all parental with me. He obviously thinks I can't take care of myself."

"I think he's sweet. Luke says he's a good guy."

"He's not my . . . type."

"Miss Picky," Kandy teased.

Lacey yawned. "Right now I'm only interested in Mr. Sandman. You two have fun. I'll see you Monday, Kandy. Thanks for calling."

"Anytime, boss."

Lacey listened to the soft click of the phone. At least one of us is lucky in love, she thought, stifling another yawn. Thankfully, Sunday morning was her snooze-in morning. *All I want is a good night's sleep.* Her wrists no longer throbbing, Lacey slipped out of her newly christened "unlucky dress" and crawled between cool sheets. She would worry about Hank *and* Jared some other time.

SIX

. . . Lacey rolled over, pulling the sheet to her chin. "What are you doing here?"

"I was worried about you." Jared's voice sounded velvety and far away, soft and soothing.

She stared into eyes the color of clouds gathering before a spring storm. There was a blatant invitation in their smoldering depths. She reached up to run her fingers through his hair, hair the color of chocolate. His left eyebrow rose a fraction and he gave her a smile that sent her pulse racing.

A summer breeze fluttered gossamer curtains and candlelight flickered deliciously. A romantic glow bathed the room.

"Turn over and let me rub your back. You look tense," he whispered.

Lacey found it impossible not to return his disarming smile, then quickly heeded his request, repositioning herself on her stomach. She wrapped her hair in a quick knot at the top of her head.

Apricots. She smelled apricots.

Next, the sound of his hands rubbing together—slick, slippery sounds. "I'll warm the lotion a little for you."

She murmured her thanks, moving her arms to her sides as he readjusted the sheet to drape at her waist. Soon all she felt were his hands, slick with lotion, sliding in even, languid strokes up her spine and down her arms. He kneaded her shoulders and neck until she groaned with pleasure.

"That's better, isn't it?"

She didn't respond at once; her tongue felt thick. She searched for words. "Your hands are amazing."

He continued with steady, gentle strokes until every patch of skin above her waist tingled with delight. Gently he pulled the sheet down, down, down. His intimate touch moved to rub her thighs. Then her calves.

"Your curves are beautiful," he whispered.

Quivering warmth began to pool in her womanly depths. Her thoughts became one wish: that he would touch her . . . *there.*

As if he could read her thoughts, Lacey felt the whisper of a touch between her thighs. Jared's hands spread her legs further apart. She didn't resist.

"So soft, so sweet . . ." he whispered.

She felt a dizzying tingle that quickly escalated. Suddenly she was soaring, riding lovely spasms, rejoicing at the attainment of her wishes.

Lacey's eyes flew open. "Wait," she called to the dark. Her blood throbbed in her veins as she suddenly remembered the intimacy of her dream, her legs still shaking from her recent dream-climax. She closed her eyes, wanting to return to the dream . . . to him.

Lacey tossed and turned the rest of the night, finally giving up on the idea of sleeping in when the first light of day filled her bedroom. Feeling a strange combination of frustration and satisfaction, she got up, exercised, showered, and made herself a huge breakfast. She indulged in a veggie scramble, steamed potatoes, freshly squeezed orange juice, and a full pot of Kona coffee.

"There's enough here for two men and a boy," she grumbled to herself as she dished up the food. She'd always found it difficult to cook for one, her refrigerator perpetually filled with plastic containers of dibs and dabs of leftovers.

Determined to forget her Saturday night experience at the club *and* her sexy dream, Lacey filled her day with old movies, buttered popcorn, and chatty phone calls to friends and relatives.

That night she slept a restful, dreamless sleep, and she felt like she was back on track by the next morning.

"Have you heard anything?" Kandy asked.

"Are you serious?" Lacey deliberately put as much sarcasm in her voice as she could.

She and Kandy were in the stockroom of the salon, sorting dozens of bottles of hair color and retail products that had just arrived. A thankful, mindless task to fill the rest of the afternoon, she thought. Perfect.

The auction rehearsal was in two hours and she had no idea if Hank would be there. Time would tell. Since her hostile altercation with him, she hadn't been back to the Rockin' Ranch, and he had made no attempt to contact her.

Her stomach tightened, recalling the repugnant incident with graphic detail. Even though she had stopped blaming herself, she wanted desperately to learn from it, forcing herself to analyze her actions, trying to determine how it could have been prevented.

"I need music." Lacey reached past Kandy to switch on a portable radio she'd bought for the salon. She didn't want to talk about Hank any more, didn't want to think about him any more. She knew thinking about it would darken her mood, and even if she had lost all enthusiasm for the Bachelor Auction, she really didn't want to spoil it for Kandy. She and *her* cowboy were doing just fine.

Kandy bounced to the oldies music and they silently worked their way through the cartons of inventory. When the music paused for an hourly news break, Lacey reached to change the station.

"And at a local country music hot spot called the Rockin' Ranch—"

Lacey's hand stopped in midair.

"—local resident, Hank Erickson, was arrested without incident for suspected credit card fraud. A part-time employee at the club, he allegedly used customer's credit card receipts to purchase a three-day cruise to Ensenada, as well as to fund a shopping spree at a men's store at a nearby mall. Now, here's Chuck with the weekend forecast . . ."

Lacey snapped off the radio. "Well, I guess that answers your question about good ol' Hank. Sounds like he had a pretty good dream date planned for us, though . . . *darn.*"

Kandy's eyes widened at Lacey's reaction.

Lacey sensed Kandy's confused discomfort. "Thank

goodness I don't have to deal with that low life." She gently punched Kandy in the forearm. "Lighten up, will ya? It's not the end of the world."

"You're right. So *what* if we're short one cowboy," Kandy agreed.

Lacey felt the weight of the world lift from her shoulders. It was always easier dealing with a known than an unknown. Now she knew Hank would not be at the rehearsal and hopefully there wouldn't be too much hassle if the event was minus one cowboy bachelor.

"I'm your sister, Jared, talk to me."

Joann glared at him from across the kitchen table, her voice calm but insistent. His sister was known more for her tendency to bulldoze her way through life than for her ability to "wait patiently and see."

"Jared, I know you better than you know yourself. Something's eating at you. The last time I saw you like this you were deciding whether or not to propose marriage to that—"

Jared's scowl stopped his sister from finishing the sentence. He watched as her eyes widened.

"Okay, fess up. Who is she?"

"Why do you assume it's about a woman? Geez!"

"It is, isn't it?" Joann's face brightened with a huge grin. "Okay, let me see. Someone at the club? Waitress? Fan?"

"Stop it. Can you be serious?"

Joann nodded, her grin disappearing instantly. "Jared, just tell me about it. We can do this, you know."

Jared sat at the kitchen table, carefully placing a glass of iced tea in front of his sister. "I'm sorry Jo. I'm just not used to feeling like this."

"Like what?"

Jared closed his eyes for a moment, then stared out the window to avoid his sister's scrutiny. "At the club, I met the woman who cut Jamie's hair."

"You met Lacey? Really? This is getting interesting already—paths crossing paths and all. She sure had Jamie wrapped around her little finger that day."

Jared sighed. Why was it so hard to just talk about it? He proceeded with his explanation, choosing his words carefully. He knew his sister was right, the whole business of Lacey and Hank was consuming him. "She was interested in this jerk from the club. I found out she asked him to be in some charity bachelor auction at the mall and I decided to warn her about him and—"

"Now she's pissed at you for interfering, right?"

Jared nodded. Obviously a girl thing, he thought. "I don't *want* to be interested in her, Jo. I like things just the way they are, but—"

"Things could be better."

"What do you mean?"

"Jamaica's going to need a woman around—at least a role model other than her wonderful auntie, you know. What's wrong with at least entertaining the idea? What are you afraid of?"

"Don't get all touchy-feely with me, Jo, you know better than that. Jamie and I are doing fine."

"Yes, you are. So, what exactly is the problem?" She paused, seemingly lost in thought. "There's more, isn't there?"

"I drove her home the other night and we left things a little awkward."

"So, go apologize."

"But I didn't *do* anything—"

"Doesn't matter. If something's bothering you, it sounds like you at least need to clear the air. You don't have to show up with flowers or anything, just go to the mall and buy her a cup of coffee. Talk. Make nice."

Jared groaned. She was right. No matter what, he hated the feeling of unresolved conflict and he'd vowed to never live like that again. His marriage had been one conflict after another and if he hadn't learned anything else, he'd learned that.

"Look, little brother, I'll stay with Jamaica and you go down the mountain and get it over with. You might as well," she teased, "because you're going to stew about it anyway. Go on."

Jared's chair scraped loudly against the wood floor as he pushed himself away from the table. He leaned down to plant a kiss on his sister's cheek before he strolled out the door. He hated when she was right, but had to admit he was starting to feel better already.

Lacey's head was bowed over a huge stack of client receipts as she added the week's totals a third time. *Why am I having so much trouble?* She glanced at the clock—still an hour before closing time.

After the last two clients of the evening had canceled, she generously let everyone else go home a little early. Foot traffic in the mall was slow, and it didn't look like there would be a last minute Friday night walk-in after all.

She slowed down her fingers, preventing them from flying over the keys of the adding machine. She felt uneasy, distracted. *Damn.*

The auction rehearsal had gone well the night before and the mall's marketing manager had listened sympathetically to her tale of woe about her missing cowboy, though she *had* implied she really wished Lacey would try to find a last minute replacement.

She sucked in her cheeks, nervously biting them as she pressed the total key. Balanced at last. *Last minute replacement? Right. Maybe I should just plan on asking the next male customer.* She shook her head, murmuring, "I can't wait for this whole thing to be over."

"Hi, Lacey."

She jumped, startled at the voice, and looked up.

Jared returned her stare. He had quietly walked into the reception area of the salon, watching her bowed head for a few moments while she worked.

He gazed at her as her furrowed brow relaxed and her face slowly broke into a slight smile.

"Sorry if I interrupted you," he began. "I wondered if we could just talk for a minute."

"About what?"

Jared swallowed hard. "I wanted to . . . apologize if I offended you the other night. It's really none of my business if you and Hank—"

"Hank's in jail."

Jared froze in mid-thought. *Jail?*

"At least I don't have to see him or deal with him now," she continued. "I look at it as a gift, actually—so, no harm, no foul, right?"

Jared stared. Her voice sounded hard, with a slight tinge of embarrassment. "And the auction?"

"Missing one cowboy. Unless you'd like to fill in," she prompted. "The show's tomorrow night at seven."

"I don't think that's my style. Besides, no one likes to be second choice," he said with mock severity.

Lacey's smile flattened into a straight line. Her fingers drummed nervously on the desk.

"Look," he began, "about Hank . . . I just think you need to take time to know someone before you make assumptions about them."

"Are you talking about Hank or you?"

Jared didn't answer. Already their conversation felt like the beginnings of an argument.

Her face softened. "Jared, I'm sorry. I'm just feeling mad and disappointed."

Jared nodded.

"And I'm just stubborn enough to wish you weren't right."

The sound of giggling interrupted Jared's reply and he watched Lacey's demeanor change from friendly to professional. "Excuse me, it looks like I have some business."

Jared glanced at two teenaged girls who huddled in the doorway behind him.

"Thanks for stopping by, Jared."

Jared didn't answer her cool dismissal. He left the salon and retraced his steps back to his truck, breathing in the cool evening air as though he couldn't quite get enough oxygen into his lungs.

Why does she make me feel like a punk kid? I'm too old for this. He shook his head, more than a little annoyed at the tightness in his jeans. How could he be attracted to someone he couldn't even have a normal conversation with?

SEVEN

Lacey nervously bit the ragged edge of her thumbnail. The charity auction was starting. Kandy had put the finishing touches on Luke's hair and had even persuaded him to let her dab a little face powder on his nose.

"Doesn't he look yummy?" Kandy fanned herself with her hand. Her gaze followed Luke as he joined the line of men waiting to be introduced.

Lacey agreed. "He looks wonderful. You did a great job, Kandy. Nice hair."

"Thanks. Sorry it didn't work out for you and Hank."

"Don't be. I just feel bad that Luke has to be the only cowboy."

"But he's not."

Lacey whirled at the sound of Jared's voice.

"Lacey, darling, look what *I* found." The sickeningly sweet voice of the marketing manager interrupted her thoughts. "*Your* cowboy is here after all."

Lacey simply stared at Jared.

"He does belong to you, doesn't he, honey?"

"No . . . yes . . . what are you doing here?"

"You look great, Jared," Kandy said.

Lacey stared at him. He was devastatingly handsome, dressed in a black leather blazer, crisp white shirt, and black string tie. His brown hair looked like polished mahogany in the bright backstage lighting; the silver strands at his temples were more noticeable, adding dazzling highlights. Her gaze dropped to his waist, which sported a stunning silver and turquoise belt buckle above snug black jeans. His familiar black boots had been recently polished. He looked taller. Different.

"What do you think, Lacey, *with* the hat or *without* it?" Jared asked.

She looked up, her pulse throbbing at her temples, embarrassed to have him catch her downward gaze. "Let me see it on."

Jared tipped his head forward and placed a black felt hat on his head.

She stepped forward, instinctively smoothing his hair behind his ears and pulling out a few strands that were tucked inside his collar. *Apricots.* Why did he have to smell so good?

"Surprised?" Jared whispered.

"What made you change your mind?" she replied.

"Truth?"

"It'd be nice."

"My big sister."

Lacey laughed. Maybe things would be all right after all. *We just have to get through the evening.* "Thanks to your sister, then. I'd like to meet her." Lacey continued to straighten and smooth Jared's tie and collar.

"You've already met."

"You're kidding. Where?"

"Do you remember a little girl named Jamie? Jamaica? My sister brought her in and you fixed her hair."

"She was *your* Jamie?"

Jared nodded. "And I can hardly get her to take off that damn princess hat you gave her, by the way. I think there's glitter in every room of the house."

Lacey took a step back. "You should fetch a good price," she teased. She watched as Jared's face seemed to pale as if he suddenly remembered the reason he was there.

He groaned. "I can't believe I'm doing this."

"It'll be over soon. I've got to go. You can join Luke in line. Unfortunately, you two are up last."

Jared tipped his head in the direction of Luke, who was giving him a thumbs up.

"Don't worry, the ladies will love you." Lacey felt

a sudden heat in her cheeks. They would love him, she realized, and he probably *would* fetch a good price. *I sound barbaric.*

Kandy whispered, "Lacey, the girls from the shop have a spot saved up front. You coming?"

"You go on, Kandy. I'm going to run over to the salon for a few minutes and I'll meet you after it's over."

Kandy's face drew into a pout. "You're no fun. Aren't you even going to bid on anyone?"

Lacey groaned. "Do you have enough money to buy your cowboy? You need to borrow any?"

"I'm fine, thanks. I've been saving tips all week. See ya." Her face brightened as she twirled to join the crowd.

The sound of someone tapping on a microphone drew Lacey's attention to the stage.

"Is this on? Can everyone hear me out there?" The master of ceremonies was a local radio personality whose voice was unmistakable. She listened to his familiar mellow baritone.

"Good evening, everyone. My name is Gabe Freeman from KGLD, San Diego's number one Golden Oldies radio. Calm down ladies, the bidding is about to begin. Welcome to the first annual "Bachelor For Sale" charity auction." His voice was quickly drowned out by the noisy crowd.

Lacey scanned the stage. It was a good-looking group of men. The charity should do well tonight, she thought.

Gabe raised his hands in attempts to control the crowd, continuing, "Remember that your kind donations this evening will benefit our local Pediatric Aids fund. And don't forget that tonight's highest bidder will join her bachelor on a Dream Date, donated by

Adventure Tours, right here at the Wentworth Mall. So think big and bid big!"

"Good luck, Kandy," Lacey whispered as she left the shrieking crowd behind her.

Stifling a yawn, Lacey checked her watch. She hated crunching numbers but at least now she wouldn't have to come in early tomorrow to prepare her monthly report.

Locking the salon door behind her, she walked to the mall's courtyard where the stage was still full, though the crowd had tamed down considerably. On the stage, all the men except for Luke and Jared had a woman draped on his left arm.

Lacey made her way to the side of the crowd, hoping to squeeze into a space toward the front. Luke was up next.

Kandy's familiar squeal caught her attention. The bidding was intense, but brisk, and Kandy was victorious.

"Mr. Luke Anderson has been purchased for the highest price of the night by the lady in red. Please join us on stage, madam. Congratulations. You two will win the Dream Date unless this last bachelor can fetch a higher bid."

Lacey's gaze returned to the stage as Jared walked to the auction platform. She felt a twinge of . . . regret? Jealousy? She wasn't sure. He did look especially attractive. Maybe even a little dangerous. *Not my type,* she reminded herself. He's got a kid. He's divorced. Older.

Her stare glued to Jared now standing next to the emcee, she folded her arms against her chest. *You're not for me.*

The marketing director slid up next to her, grabbing her elbow. "Lacey, darling, aren't you bidding on your cowboy?"

"Nope." The word barely escaped her clenched jaws. Taking a deep breath, she continued, "Did the charity do well tonight?" Lacey's gaze didn't budge from the stage.

"Oh, this has been the event of the century," she said. "We've raised over eight thousand dollars already, and television cameras have even shown up. We're getting great publicity."

A loud cheer from the crowd interrupted their conversation. Lacey stepped up on tiptoe to try to see who was bidding on Jared.

"Oh, my!" the marketing director squealed. "That woman over there just doubled the last bid!"

Lacey looked at a woman at the front of the crowd. She looked slightly familiar, but she couldn't quite place her. Her gaze shifted to Jared's face. He looked relieved. Did he know her?

As if reading her thoughts, the marketing director asked, "Do you think they know each other?"

"Maybe."

Gabe shouted to the crowd, "Will anyone increase the bid? Going once, twice, *sold* to the lady in the front."

Lacey examined the expression on Jared's face. He looked genuinely happy. His grin looked . . . mischievous.

"Well, our final bachelor has fetched the highest price of the evening and will be escorting his date on an all-expense-paid weekend at a secluded, romantic mountain getaway. Help the lady up to the stage, please."

The mystery woman stopped at the steps to the

stage and gestured to the emcee. Gabe covered his microphone with one hand and leaned down in order to hear her.

Standing up, he announced to the crowd, "Ladies and gentlemen, I have been informed that the winning bidder has purchased this last bachelor as a gift for someone. Would Lacey Murdock please join us on stage to claim her man and to accept the "Dream Date of the Evening?" Where are you, Lacey? Your cowboy is waiting."

Lacey felt a hand in the small of her back as the marketing director gave her a substantial shove.

"Here she is! Here she is!"

Jared's gaze locked for a moment on hers, then Lacey forced a smile and made her way up the steps to the stage. Gabe took her hand and guided her to a spot on the platform next to Jared.

"I had no idea—" Jared started to explain.

"Who *was* that woman?"

"My lovely *ex*-sister, Joann," he answered through clenched teeth.

The spotlight from a camera glared in her face as the emcee stuck his microphone under her chin. "We're going live now for Channel 7 News," he whispered. "Miss Murdock—it *is* Miss, isn't it?"

Lacey commanded her weak smile to remain. "Yes."

"And how do you feel about winning this eligible bachelor."

Please let me say something intelligent. She took a breath and counted to three. "I'm so pleased that the Pediatric Aids charity did so well tonight, thanks to this event. The Wentworth Mall should be proud to be a part of raising funds for such a worthy cause."

"And Mr. Conrad, are you really a cowboy?" Gabe asked, tipping the microphone toward Jared.

He grimaced. Might as well take advantage of the opportunity for a plug. "I grew up on a Colorado cattle ranch and after I moved to southern California, I started raising llamas. I own Harmony Ranch and breed llamas for pack and fiber."

"Well," Gabe continued, "I guess we can't always assume a cowboy wrangles cows, can we?"

Jared winced. He hoped Marsha wasn't watching the news. He could imagine the sound of her always demeaning laughter. She'd been embarrassed by his choice to work with llamas—it wasn't her idea of a "real" ranch. He glanced at Lacey, trying to read her reaction.

"Don't they make a handsome couple?" Gabe asked the crowd, urging their applause as he nudged Lacey and Jared closer together. "Big smiles for the television cameras," he coaxed.

The crowd cheered as they too turned to face the cameras, waving furiously in hopes of being seen on the eleven o'clock news.

Lacey felt Jared's arm settle at her waist. It felt good. Too good.

"Lacey, I'm really sorry." His voice sounded sincere.

"Don't worry about it."

"Maybe there's some way we can get out of the . . . the date part," he whispered

"With any luck." An unexpected lump rose in her throat. She knew it wasn't likely, well aware of the publicity opportunity that was attached to the evening's Dream Date prize. The mall's marketing director had secured newspaper coverage for the

Dream Date, plus the charity was counting on the extra promotional attention. It was a package deal.

"Lacey?"

"Right now, Jared, let's just keep smiling for the cameras. We'll figure things out later."

When the cameras finally stopped flashing and the reporters were gone, Jared left Lacey with Kandy and Luke and went in search of his sister.

When he spotted her in the courtyard next to the stage, he could feel a vein in his neck throbbing with the instant rise in his blood pressure.

"Pretty pleased with yourself, aren't you, Jo?"

Joann flashed a smile reminiscent of their teen years. They'd fought like cats and dogs, but even then she'd had a habit of somehow getting what she wanted in the end.

"Man, you should have seen your face—"

Jared cut her off. "Where's Jamie?"

"Mom's got her. Before I left, though, I told her you'd have a surprise to tell her tomorrow. She's pretty excited."

Jared shook his head. How had this happened?

Joann gave his shoulder a good-natured jab. "Hey, jerk, you were worth every penny. Why don't you just go on this Dream Date and have a little fun?"

"Because I don't want—" Jared stopped himself. He took a moment to collect his thoughts. "Because, dear sister, she isn't the type of woman I would *want*—"

"—*if* you were looking, and you're not," she finished.

"Jared?"

He turned at the sound of Lacey's voice and gestured for her to join them.

Joann extended her hand. "Hi, Lacey, I'm Joann. Hope you're not as mad at me as my little brother."

"Mostly surprised, actually," Lacey replied. She stood next to Jared, close enough to feel his body heat. She was tired, her feet hurt, and she had to be at the salon bright and early in the morning. She was beginning to wonder if the night would ever end.

As if on cue, Joann said her goodbyes, leaving them alone.

Awkwardly, Jared cleared his throat and muttered uneasily, "Where are the others?"

"Kandy and Luke went to The Cantina to celebrate."

"Got any ideas?" he grumbled.

Lacey looked up at him. His voice sounded cranky but his eyes looked almost *inviting*. Was she reading more into them than was there? "Unfortunately, I do feel obligated to go through with this for the charity's sake. They're really counting on the extra publicity."

They said nothing for a few moments.

"Sounds like a nice place," he said.

"What?"

"The bed and breakfast—the Dream Date."

"Oh, right." She nodded, remembering how thrilled the marketing manager had been to have secured a weekend at a secluded, pricey bed and breakfast in the nearby Cuyamaca mountains. She'd told her the cabins were large, cozy, and *romantic*, a favorite for local honeymooners. It had sounded like the perfect spot. *What am I thinking?*

Jared interrupted her thoughts. "Maybe what we need is a chaperon. A short, red-headed one."

Lacey looked up. Featherlike laugh lines crinkled around his gray eyes. "That would help," she said.

"Jamie would enjoy the woods," he added, "and she already thinks you're some kind of magician. It might be fun."

"Deal," she said, watching the play of emotions on his face. Did he really think it would be fun, or was he just humoring her?

"You want to ride together or meet there?" he asked, matter-of-factly.

"Together is fine." No need to take two cars, she thought. With Jamie sitting between them, everything would be fine. A perfect solution.

Lacey sighed, the strain between them now reduced. "Why don't the two of you pick me up at the salon on Saturday morning. I'll talk to the mall office and get details about the publicity and we can get this thing over with as soon as possible."

"Agreed. See you then." He tipped his hat to her and turned to leave.

Lacey stared as he walked away. There was no backward glance from him. She bit her cheek thoughtfully. *There goes one confusing man. Just when I thought I had you figured out, you have to go and be nice to me.*

At least with Jamie along, she thought, it would be easier to pass the time. Jared and his daughter could go explore the woods and she could have two days of rest and relaxation. She could definitely use the break in her routine and a weekend off was sounding better and better. *Until Saturday, then.*

Jared sat in his truck with his eyes closed for a few moments. His feelings were a tangle of confusion, his groin, painfully tight. How in hell was he going to survive a weekend with a woman who had somehow broken through his defenses?

He gripped the steering wheel tightly with both hands. *Damn.* His good-intentioned, meddling sister had very nicely managed to complicate his life. Two days and one night. That's all he had to get through. Then he would be able to separate himself from Lacey. Things would be normal again.

"Fat chance," he muttered.

EIGHT

Jared stamped his feet on the porch just outside his back door. "I'm coming. Geez!" Why did the phone always ring the minute he was occupied with the animals? It never failed. Satisfied the majority of the dirt was off his boots, he flung open the door and grabbed the wall phone. "Hello!"

"Jared, did I call at a bad time?" His sister's voice had a sugary sweet sound.

"Hey, Joann. Sorry, I was outside."

"You want me to call back later?"

He exhaled loudly, gathering his patience. "What's up?"

"I was thinking that since Jamie's going with you two to the cabin this weekend that we all might get together *before* Saturday."

"And do what?"

"Well, eat or something. I just think you might have a better time if all of you got to know each other better and—"

"Joann, just get to the point." He loved his sister dearly, but she was a master at beating around the bush. He'd learned to preserve his sanity by getting her to cut to the chase.

"Okay. I thought we could barbecue at your house. That way, you—and Jamie—would feel more comfortable and maybe things wouldn't be as awkward. And I'm sure Lacey would feel better about it, too."

Jared knew his sister too well. "You already asked her, didn't you?"

Silence answered his question.

"I've already bought the steaks, and some sweet corn from that produce stand you like," Joann said.

"You're impossible. And what night are we having this little get-together, may I ask?"

"Well, tonight, actually. How's six o'clock sound?"

"Jo—"

"I figured I better not give you a chance to say no, that's all."

Jared ran his fingers through his hair. So much for the animals, he thought. Dolly and the others would have to wait. He mentally made a quick list of chores. Clean the grill, sweep the porch and patio, an early bath for Jamie . . .

Joann interrupted his thoughts. "Lacey's bringing a salad. You got any wine to chill?"

"I'm hanging up the phone now, big sister."

"See ya," she said.

Jared's irritation quickly transformed into an abrupt case of the jitters. Unconsciously he pushed his fist into his stomach, trying to grind the butterflies in his stomach into submission. "Who cares what she thinks of our place." His glance around the kitchen caused him to add mopping the floor to his growing list.

Walking out the back door, he stood at the top step. "Jamie, come in the house, now. We're having company and I need your help."

He watched as his daughter appeared at the barn door, a kitten under each arm.

"Coming, Daddy. Let me put the kitties back and I'll be right there." Her high-pitched honeyed voice tranquilized him. In two hours, Lacey would be there. In *their* house. In *their* home.

An hour of straightening, another to clean themselves, and they were finished. Jared paced the front porch, staring at the driveway for the first sign of a car. Jamie put the finishing touches on her room. When he'd caught her pushing all her toys under the bed, he'd insisted she utilize her toy box. She was a good kid, easy to like. He wondered if Lacey liked her.

"Daddy, I'm done, come see."

"Be right there, sweetpea." On his way through the kitchen he grabbed a bottle of white Zinfandel and put it in the refrigerator. Maybe a little wine was a good idea.

Lacey checked the freeway traffic in her rearview mirror, quickly changing lanes so she wouldn't lose sight of Joann's blue Camaro. Jared's sister was a convincing woman.

After a few minutes of logical persuasion, Lacey had agreed it probably *was* a good idea to have a casual dinner with Jared and Jamie before spending the weekend with them. It became more and more obvious that Joann's meddling was rooted in her concern for her brother and niece.

She flipped the mirror open on her visor. Her face was purposely devoid of makeup except for a little lipstick. No reason to dress up, she'd convinced herself. She wore faded jeans and a denim shirt. Just a friendly meal to release some pressure in a potentially tense situation, she reminded herself.

Not my type. Not my type. Her new mantra matched the thumping beat of the ridges in the road.

As Joann cut back into the slow lane, her turn signal continued to blink. Lacey followed her off the next exit, feeling her tires shimmy as they drove onto the rutted, washboard road. Two signs flashed by: Not a Through Street, and You Are Entering the Cleveland National Forest.

"What we are entering is the boonies," she murmured. Her foot sought the brake as the quality of the road steadily diminished.

Flicking off the air conditioning, she lowered her window. Soon the pungent aroma of sage displaced the filtered air in her car. Lacey breathed deeply and filled her lungs with the fragrance and propped her elbow on the window's edge, dangling her fingers outside. She had forgotten how different the air was in the mountains. Each lungful encouraged her to relax a little more.

She focused her attention on Joann's car as it crept along several yards ahead of her, then noticed the turn signal was blinking. She followed her onto a road that had a steadily increasing upward grade and, as they climbed, Lacey noted the change in the terrain. More boulders, less trees, more short, squat shrubs.

As she followed the Camaro around a sharp curve,

the drab green and gray of the underbrush was replaced by startling patches of vibrant color. Wildflowers bordered the final stretch of what she supposed was a driveway, vibrant yellow sunflowers, orange poppies, and pink and white daisies.

Her gaze went to the end of the driveway where an odd-looking round, geodesic dome house stood. Next to it was an obviously much older, weathered gray barn that had spacious fenced pens on either side of it. Several llamas were lined up along the fence, watching her, their eyes looking curious and somehow intelligent.

She saw Jared standing on the front porch, arms crossed, feet apart. His hand lifted in a stiff wave.

"I can do this, I can do this," Lacey chanted.

As both cars came to a stop, Jared had already walked halfway to the parking area to help with the groceries. "Can you manage?" he asked Lacey, nodding at the Tupperware in her arms.

"I'm fine, thanks."

"Jo, will you do the nickel tour and I'll start the steaks?"

"Sure thing. Where's Jamaica?"

"Probably deciding what Barbie and Ken need to wear to this little shindig." His sarcasm was met with Joann's scrunched face and a grin from Lacey.

"C'mon Lacey, you'll love the house. Did you know Jared built it? He sent for one of those dome house kits. Cute, isn't it?"

Jared grimaced. Already his sister sounded like she was peddling him. And for what? he wondered. This was just a simple dinner. A chance to break the ice. Get comfortable with a woman he was about to spend the weekend with. *Stop thinking about it,* he commanded himself.

While Jared busied himself with the grill, Lacey followed Joann around the porch to the back door.

"Here's the kitchen. We can put your salad in the fridge." Before she put it away she peeked under the cover. "Looks luscious. Jared's a good cook, by the way."

Lacey returned her smile. *This is beginning to sound like a sales job.* Perhaps she was wrong about Jared's sister. Perhaps her good-natured meddling was more serious than she thought.

"Auntie Jo!" The musical sound of Jamie's voice broke the silence. "Come see my room. It's *clean.* Daddy made me."

"Jamaica, say hello to Lacey. You remember her from the salon at the mall, right?"

Jamie nodded, slipping her tiny hand in Lacey's. At the innocent welcoming touch, Lacey felt her tension loosen. She allowed the little girl to lead her to her room, only half-listening to Joann's sparse description of rooms they passed on the way.

Jamie's room was frilly, girlish. A brass trundle bed was filled with white eyelet pillows, and matching curtains draped the window. The walls were pale pink instead of the dark wood paneling that filled the rest of the house. The room definitely had a woman's touch.

"Come see my c'llections." Jamie pulled her to the window, pointing at the array of rocks, twigs and feathers that filled every space of the wide windowsill.

"It's a very nice collection," she said.

Joann joined them at the window. "Jamie's mom did the room. I don't think she ever admitted she produced a bit of a tomboy," she whispered.

Lacey stole another glance around the room. It was actually a mixture of frilly things and practical things.

The large wooden toy box looked homemade and sturdy; a well-worn braided rug covered most of the floor. Ballerinas and castles decorated most of the walls, as well as ponies and kittens.

"You like kids?" Joann asked.

"Sure . . . I guess."

"Jamie's great. We spend a lot of time together, don't we, sweetie? Why don't you go ask your dad how much longer before we eat, okay?" Jamie skipped out of the room.

"She seems great," Lacey said.

"Look," Joann started, "I'm not really here to push you two together." She laughed. "Well, I sort of am. I just thought you might . . . like each other. Jamie sure likes you."

Lacey folded her arms across her chest while Joann fluffed a pillow nervously.

"And Jared's been alone for a while now and, well, I just thought it might be interesting to see what happened."

"Look, Joann, to tell you the truth, I'm not looking for a relationship with a single dad, so I figure we should just get through this as pleasantly as possible and be done with it." Lacey listened to the tone in her own voice, hoping she didn't sound ungrateful or bitchy.

Joann's eyes widened slightly. "Hey, whatever, right? You can't blame a sister for trying."

"No harm done," Lacey replied, touching Joann's arm. "It should be a great weekend. I'm looking forward to it, actually."

Joann's face broke into a relieved grin.

"And I never thanked you properly for your donation to the charity," Lacey continued. "It was a generous bid."

"Happy to do it. Anything to shake up my little brother's life. It was worth it just to see the look on his face."

Jamie bounded into the room. "Daddy says the grub's on." Her tiny hand stifled a very pleased giggle at her father's crude phrase. "He says to bring the salad and the wine. Follow me."

Joann and Lacey obediently followed Jamie into the kitchen, stopping to gather the rest of the things they needed for their supper.

"We're eating in the brand new gazebo," Jamie directed. "Daddy just finished making it."

A wooden table was set for four, complete with flowered tablecloth and brightly colored plastic picnicware. Three plates were filled with sizzling T-bones and one plate featured a hamburger, bun, and chips. Lacey placed the salad bowl next to the platter of sweet corn in the middle of the table.

"It looks wonderful, Jared. Thanks for doing all this."

He sent a quick glare toward his sister, then flashed a smile at Lacey. She seemed genuinely pleased at his efforts.

"Ditto," said Joann.

"Lacey, why don't you sit by Jamie. Joann, you're by me."

Joann wrinkled her nose.

It was obvious to Jared that Joann had planned to have him sit next to Lacey. *No such luck, sister.* He flashed her a victor's grin.

Jared watched Lacey help Jamie get settled as they each sat down. "Dig in, everyone, before the bugs hear we're having dinner." Jamie giggled and took an enormous bite out of her burger, chewing with great exaggeration.

"Take it easy, Jamie. I was just kidding." Jared glanced at Lacey, who was apparently comfortable eating outside. Quite the contrast, he thought, knowing that his ex-wife would have insisted he mosquito-net the entire gazebo before she would have ever consented to eat outdoors.

Lacey helped herself to an ear of corn, closing her eyes as she bit into it. "I think this is the freshest corn I've had all season. Just picked?" she asked.

"Well, I picked it up on the way here tonight," Joann answered, "at that stand off the freeway on the edge of El Cajon."

Jared's gaze locked on Lacey's face. Unconsciously, he reached for her. "You have a kernel of corn on your chin," he explained.

As he delicately nudged the kernel off her chin, Jared caught his breath. It felt both absurd and natural to reach for her. He heard her quiet gasp as he touched her. She blinked. But it wasn't surprise that flickered in her eyes. Perhaps an unasked question, he thought.

"Sorry," he mumbled.

"No problem. I'd hate to be the only one sitting here with food on my chin." Her face broke into a comfortable grin.

Jared turned his attention back to his plate, his appetite suddenly gone, replaced by a slight feeling of dread. If he continued to feel such conflicting emotions, spending the weekend with Lacey would be more of a challenge than he could handle.

Outside, with no city lights to compete with them, the stars that blanketed the night sky were impressive, even to Jared. Lacey sounded awestruck as he pointed out some of the constellations to her.

She reached for his arm as they strolled to her car in the darkness, stumbling a little, unsure of her footing. Jared realized he was so used to the dark he took for granted that everyone was. Even on moonless nights he was comfortable walking around his property.

He also realized how comfortable he felt around Lacey.

Dinner had gone surprisingly well and the time had flown by. He was astounded when Jamie's bedtime had approached, signaling the end of the evening.

It had been a long time since he'd felt so at ease. He'd ignored Joann's glances of satisfaction as much as he could, though her Chesire Cat smile was almost constant throughout the evening.

"Thanks for walking me down," Lacey said. She fumbled for her keys and sat down in the car, quickly shutting the door to squelch the interior light and rolling down the window.

"Thanks for reading to Jamie." Jared put one hand on the roof of the car and leaned so he could look in the window, trying to read the expression on her face.

"Luckily, Cinderella is one of my favorites. And she's a great kid." She turned away from his steady gaze to turn the key in the ignition. "Thanks for dinner. I'll see you on Saturday morning."

"Right. Goodnight," he said softly.

Lacey looked at Jared and smiled. Was it really disappointment she saw in his eyes before he turned away? It had been such a nice evening. It felt like . . . *family*, she decided. She shuddered, trying to shake off that much too familiar feeling. It was exactly how it had felt with Blake and his son. Normal. Fun. Comfortable.

Not on your agenda, she reminded herself. Much too familiar. Warning bells rang in her head.

She put the car in reverse to turn it around and make her way down the narrow driveway. Glancing in the mirror just before she turned onto the road that would take her down off his mountain, she saw Jared's silhouette leaning against one of the porch posts, his hands deep in his pockets. *I wonder what you're thinking, Jamie's daddy.*

NINE

"You're sure you can handle my regulars?" For the fifth time, Lacey checked the appointment book, scribbling last minute notes onto stickies indicating the size of perm rods she used on Mrs. Clark, reminders to not trim Jennifer's bangs too short, and which conditioner she used for each client.

Kandy moaned. "Yes, I think I can handle your regulars. Will you just relax?"

Lacey closed her eyes for a moment, trying to lessen the growing feeling of agitation. It had been years since she'd had a Saturday off, since before she'd finished cosmetology school, she realized, and she hardly knew how to act.

"You really have everything you need in that little suitcase?" Kandy's voice was filled with disbelief.

The sound of giggling distracted Lacey, drawing

her attention to the back of the salon where two of her younger stylists stood, hands over their mouths, their heads together. She caught Kandy sending them a stern, hushing glance. *Something was up.*

"Why are you all so concerned with my bag, anyway?" She returned her gaze to the back of the salon.

"I'm not interested at all. I just thought you might want to borrow a few things for your dream date."

"It's only two days—"

"And one night," Kandy finished. Her voice had a sheepish tone.

Lacey glanced back at Kandy.

"You ready?"

Jared stood at the front counter, his voice startling her, causing an unexpected skip in her heartbeat.

"Hi, Jared. I'll get my bag and meet you outside."

"I'm parked by the theaters."

Lacey watched him leave, then walked briskly to the back of the salon for her suitcase. She sent a final parental glare to Kandy. "Stay out of trouble, ladies, and I'll see you on Monday."

Lacey walked through the mall, switching her suitcase from hand to hand a couple times before she arrived at the parking lot. It felt a lot heavier than she remembered and underscored her feeling of uneasiness. She had a hunch that the weekend was either going to be spectacular or completely unbearable. Her own emotions were an unnerving amalgamation of dread and curiosity—not a good sign.

Even though Jamie would be along to lessen the tension, she still faced two days—and one night, as Kandy had reminded her—with someone she reluctantly had to admit she found attractive. *Not your type.* The voice in her head was sounding somewhat weaker. Jared Conrad was not what was good for her, she argued, *no matter what I dream or think.*

In the crowded parking lot, Jared leaned casually against his truck until the moment he saw her. In a few quick strides he devoured the distance between them. Quickly he took the suitcase from her hand, tucking it behind the bench seat of the truck. She noticed a small leather tote and a guitar case already there.

She also noticed the absence of his daughter.

"Are we picking Jamie up on the way?" she asked.

"She's got the flu. Joann's got her."

"Why didn't you call me?" She tried to control the irritation in her voice. This was not starting out well. The picture of a chaperoned, relaxing weekend melted before her eyes.

Jared shrugged. "I figured we would end up going anyway. It seemed like a waste of time."

Lacey stared at him with skepticism. "You should have called." He should have given her the option to back out, she thought.

Jared answered her with a questioning glance.

Lacey climbed into the truck, feeling both resigned and confused. Why was she so upset? "Sorry. You're right. Let's call a truce, okay?"

"Fine with me."

They rode in suffocating silence, finally turning onto the two-lane road she knew led up the mountain to the bed and breakfast retreat.

Lacey stared out the window, lost in thought. What was she thinking? To spend the weekend with a . . . a stranger. A handsome stranger, she reminded herself. She felt like she had just set herself up for the biggest kind of trouble she could imagine.

Jared cleared his throat, breaking the silence.

"Do you know anything more about what to expect, publicity-wise?"

His words jarred her introspection, but served to bring her back to the reality of the situation. "Reporters from both the San Diego paper and a few of the smaller local papers are supposed to be there by noon."

"Am I dressed okay?" he asked.

Reluctantly, Lacey shifted sideways in her seat to look at him, tucking her multicolored gauze skirt around her knees. He was wearing dark blue jeans and a forest green, lightweight cotton shirt. His black hat was on the seat between them. They would look good together for the photos, she confessed to herself.

"Well?" His low voice was a little awkward.

"You look like a cowboy, if that's what you mean." She smiled when he threw her an exasperated glance. "You look fine. You always do."

His reaction to her compliment was a disturbing silence that continued for several miles.

"Jared?" Lacey's voice ended the quiet.

"What?"

"Are we there yet?"

A grin destroyed his concentration and Lacey saw the tense lines in his face relax.

"Feels like Jamie's here," he said.

"I wish she was."

Jared turned his head to look at her.

"How come?" he asked.

Lacey turned away to gaze out the window. "I just thought it would be fun for you two, to get away together."

"Yeah, we don't get away much."

"Because of the animals?"

Jared nodded.

Even so, Lacey envisioned his ranch as the perfect place for a child to grow up. She envied the little girl, having so much space to run and play. Jamie had told her of all her special places—the loft in the barn, her garden, a favorite climbing tree. And she had shared her love of the animals.

"Are llamas as sweet-tempered as they look?" she asked.

"They're gentle animals. Intelligent. And independent, though they don't like to live alone."

Like you? she wondered, the thought materializing, unwanted but true.

Lacey returned her gaze to the scenery, suddenly eager to keep the silence from returning. "Do you know what kind of trees these are?"

"Mostly scrub oak and manzanita." Jared slowed his speed, pointing to the side of the road. "The reddish brown trunks with the twisted branches are manzanita."

"Manzanita," she repeated.

"It means little apple in Spanish. Native Americans ate the berries raw or cooked them and ground them up."

"And the pine trees?"

"The evergreens here are mostly Coulter pine." He pointed again. "The ones with the dark gray bark and the giant pine cones." He pointed again. "And those flowers are golden yarrow."

"Mmm," she answered. "Can we turn off the air conditioning and roll down the windows?"

He obliged, adjusting a lever on the dash.

She breathed audibly. "It smells different than at your place."

"Different elevation, different plants."

"Did you plant the flowers by the driveway?" she asked.

Jared paused for a few moments, as if debating his answer. "The year Jamie was born." His voice had a tone of finality, concluding their conversation.

They rode in silence for the remainder of the trip.

Lacey rested her cheek on her arm as she leaned her head out the window to breathe in the distinct mountain fragrances. There was a sagey smell similar to what she remembered from Jared's place, but here it mingled with scents of pine and an earthy smell she couldn't identify.

There was something very soothing about mountain air, she decided. Minute by minute, she felt her anxiety subside. She realized that she had almost forgotten how to take time off. For months, her focus had been to increase the salon's clientele, surpass retail sales figures and goals, and prove her worth to the corporate office.

If nothing else, she concluded, this weekend would remind her that there was more to life than work. Her thought was interrupted with a start as she felt Jared abruptly apply the brakes. She straightened in her seat, unconsciously smoothing her hair away from her face. She had worn it loose, and the breeze from the window had caused it to curl.

She flipped down the visor, hoping for a mirror. *Not too bad.* Nothing that a little hairspray couldn't fix. She caught Jared's gaze in the mirror. He looked as nervous as she felt.

The small parking lot in front of them was crowded with cars. Jared stopped the truck near the front of the two-story stone house that faced them. A carved wooden sign hung from a post directing guests to come inside to register.

"You ready for this?" he asked.

"It shouldn't be too bad. A few pictures, a few questions. It looks like a nice place."

There were tall pine trees scattered around the house, and distinct paths wound through them that presumably led to the cabins.

An aproned woman fluttered down the stone steps of the house, waving feverishly at them.

Jared caught Lacey's stare and grinned. "And here comes Aunt Bea to meet us."

She answered with mock seriousness. "Well, I guess we better just cooperate with her and get this thing over with."

Jared raised an eyebrow. "I'll get the bags. You head the madwoman off at the pass."

Their easy banter comforted her. Lacey took a deep breath and opened her door, mentally slipping into her professional persona before her sandaled feet touched the ground.

After surviving the publicity ordeal of two photographers and four reporters, Jared and Lacey followed their hostess into the kitchen. Through Mrs. Miller's hurried, frantic monologue they learned she and her husband had lived all their married lives in the secluded stone house, year by year building enough rental cabins to make a decent living for themselves.

While Jared and Lacey listened, she bustled around the kitchen, efficiently building mile-high roast beef sandwiches. "You must be famished," she muttered. "I didn't think those reporters would ever leave."

Jared and Lacey exchanged neutral glances.

"Don't get me wrong," she continued, "the publicity is priceless—you just can't buy that kind of advertising." The woman didn't look up from her work. "Lettuce and tomato?"

Jared and Lacey said "yes" in unison.

"There. Now you two just sit here and eat. I'll check on your cabin and have Andy take your bags over." Before she left, she paused long enough to put down two plates on the table, each heaped with potato salad and a monstrous sandwich. "Help yourself to whatever's in the icebox to drink."

Unhesitatingly, Jared took a bite out of the sandwich, surprised how hungry he felt. The bread was sweet and dark, definitely homemade. It would be a treat to have someone else handle meals for a couple days, he decided.

He paused a moment and shrugged the tension from his shoulders. He felt the distinct crack of some vertebrae in his spine. It had been a very long, uncomfortable afternoon.

Three hours of posing with his arm around Lacey's waist, gazing into her green eyes, forced to stand where and how the photographers wished, arms constantly around each other; he was exhausted from the strain of restraint.

Their final pose had consisted of Lacey sitting on his lap while they stared into the fire that blazed in the gigantic stone fireplace. It had almost been too much. He wondered if she'd felt his hardened groin. If she had, she hadn't shown it, and for that he was grateful.

Surprisingly, the three hours seemed to have little, if any, effect on her. She had remained cool, calm, and collected. He had been amazed at her composure through it all, wondering how she could remain so detached.

Every time his hand was on her body he'd had to

fill his mind with distractions—lists of groceries, tools, names; anything to keep himself from caressing her arm, her shoulder, her back. It had been torturous.

Jared decided that even after hours of intimate poses, he knew less about her than he thought.

"Good?" Lacey asked, interrupting his thoughts.

He nodded, mouth too full to answer. He watched her as she took a decidedly unladylike bite of the sandwich. At least she was human enough to be hungry, he thought.

They ate silently for several moments. "I may live," he said finally.

She nodded her agreement.

Jared's chair scraped noisily as he pushed himself away from the table. He opened the refrigerator door and stuck his head inside. "There's milk, OJ, and beer."

"Beer," she answered.

He opened both beers and put them on the table. As he drew a long swallow from his, Lacey did the same.

Jared watched her, trance-like, as her tongue flicked over her lower lip to catch a tiny drop of liquid. She caught him staring, and her cheeks flushed red. "I don't usually like beer, but this is good, creamy."

He nodded. "One of the best dark beers out of Mexico." He stared at her lips, moist and full.

The slamming door signaled the return of their hostess, jolting him back to reality. He only had one thought. *It's going to be a very long night.*

TEN

Jared walked silently behind Lacey as they followed Mrs. Miller to the cabin she had selected for them. While she chattered to Lacey about the ups and downs of the bed and breakfast business, Jared stared at Lacey's hair.

Her long curls captured the intermittent rays of sunlight that broke through the pines, producing dazzling highlights of dark auburn and deep mahogany. Why was he noticing her hair, of all things, he wondered. His hand reached out to lift a curl, quickly replacing it as Lacey's hand reached back to smooth it.

I've got to get a grip. He felt suddenly self-conscious, a schoolboy ready to torment the girl he secretly desired. He forced himself to look ahead at the cabin they were approaching.

It was built of rough logs, with a large stone chimney reminiscent of the one at the main house. Pine trees grew amazingly close to the walls, sheltering it from the late afternoon sun and heat. There was a definite ambience of coziness, seclusion, and peace and quiet.

Inside the cabin, Jared and Lacey obediently followed their hostess from room to room, listening attentively.

"This one rents almost exclusively to newlyweds," she explained.

Lacey avoided looking at Jared, her pulse quickening.

At first glance their accommodations seemed like a typical rustic cabin, with its rough-hewn log walls and plank floor, but Mrs. Miller proudly pointed out all the modern amenities.

"There's plenty of wood for the fireplace. It'll get chilly as soon as the sun goes down. Matches are on the mantel. Do you know how to build a fire?"

Lacey glanced at Jared. He nodded. She wasn't so sure she *wanted* to see him by firelight.

"We just remodeled the bathroom to make room for an oversized tub in here," Mrs. Miller explained, "complete with whirlpool jets. People pay more for it these days." She pointed out the controls.

Sounds like my idea of the perfect Saturday night. Lacey gazed longingly at the huge clawfoot tub. Her muscles ached. She wasn't sure if it was from the tense ride up the mountain or from the stress of all the uncomfortably romantic poses the photographers had insisted on.

The feel of Jared's muscular arms around her had made her head swim. She had used every ounce of ability to concentrate on not reacting to the feel of his body touching hers in so many intimate poses. In her attempt to block her feelings, she barely remembered what had even happened over the three hours of dealing with the publicity crew.

"The bedroom's over here," Mrs. Miller continued, "and there's an extra comforter in the closet."

Lacey gasped in appreciation. The bedroom was filled with mint condition antiques, giving the impression of walking into a high-class nineteenth century hotel instead of a rustic mountain cabin. Wildflowers filled cranberry-glass vases on the tall dresser and bedside tables. An upholstered rocking chair sat by the window next to a round table covered with an antique lace cloth.

The hardwood floors were covered with thick, Persian carpets that begged to be walked on barefoot. In front of the fireplace was a large sheepskin rug.

The bed was an old-fashioned four-poster, open at the top, each post draped in gauzy cotton fabric. Pillows were heaped on the bed, a hand-stitched quilt completing the look.

"And here's the private patio." Mrs. Miller opened tall French doors and they followed her out to a fenced-in deck where a small hot tub was recessed in the center. Next to the spa were two oversized wicker chairs and a glass-topped table.

"It's beautiful," Lacey said.

Jared stood in the doorway, his arms folded across his chest.

"I'm so glad you kids like it." Mrs. Miller clicked her tongue graciously. "No television and no phone. You two just relax and enjoy yourselves. The cabin comes with a gourmet breakfast in a basket, so check your front stoop after eight tomorrow morning. There's a coffee maker in the kitchenette and a fridge that the auction people stocked for you. Have a good evening."

Before Lacey could respond, Mrs. Miller bustled past Jared and out the front door.

He remained in the doorway, watching. Lacey bent, lifting the edge of the hot tub cover. Steam escaped into the air. "It's already hot."

"Sometimes it's more energy efficient to keep it heated all the time. You bring a suit?" he asked.

Lacey swished her hand in the water. The temperature felt perfect. "I didn't think I'd need one." She glanced at him, anticipating his next comment.

"Me neither. You wanna flip for it? Bathtub or hot tub?"

Lacey smiled at his diplomatic solution. "Nah. I'll take the bathtub. All I have is a shower at home. A bubble bath sounds perfectly decadent to me."

"Let me use the facilities. I'll grab a towel and be out of your way in a jiff."

She wondered how many hours she could soak in a hot bath before she withered away. Seemed a perfect way to kill some of the evening, she decided. Walking inside, she located her suitcase, and with a groan, managed to heave it up on the bed. When she unzipped the main compartment, she discovered a bottle of champagne and an envelope.

"It's got to be Kandy," she said as she ripped open the envelope to read the note inside: *Remember, girls just* ought *to have fun! Don't worry, Lacey, we've got everything under control. You concentrate on relaxing—hope the bubbly helps! Love, the Girls.*

Lacey pulled out the bottle of champagne, then a basket of wonderfully fragrant soaps and lotions from her favorite bath shop at the mall. She brought them closer to her nose. Strawberries, she decided. A small bottle of bubble bath completed the gift pack.

"I'm done. It's all yours," Jared called from the hall.

"Thanks. See you in a few hours." She looked up to see Jared's head at the doorway.

"You're joking, right?"

"I plan to soak until it's not fun anymore. I'm just not sure how long that'll be."

"Right. You need any help in here?" His gaze was on the bottle and gift basket.

"Oh, the girls at the salon sent a few surprises in my suitcase."

He grinned at her. "I like surprises. See ya."

Lacey stared after him. Why were they getting along so well all of a sudden? She frowned.

Turning her attention back to her suitcase, she located her makeup bag and bathroom paraphernalia. "Okay, where are my pajamas?" She dug through her entire suitcase with no success. At the very bottom, she heard the rustle of paper.

"What now?" She pulled out a tissue-wrapped bundle, quickly tearing into the thin paper. Inside was a long white nightgown and matching sheer, white robe. The silky material was whisper light and extraordinarily soft. It was a beautiful ensemble. *Great. I think I will have to kill them all when I get back.* She placed the set back into her suitcase, settling for a sweatshirt and jeans to put on after her bath.

On the deck, Jared closed the doors behind him and slipped out of his clothes. He imagined Lacey was doing the same thing at that moment. He clenched his teeth and stepped into the steaming water of the hot tub, then let his body go limp and slid completely into the water, head and all.

A small groan escaped his throat as he pulled his head out of the water, wiping his eyes and smoothing back his hair. Settling himself on the smooth bench that circled the interior, he cradled his neck on the edge of the tub.

With great effort, he emptied his mind of every nagging thought, every chore that wasn't being done, each detail of his normal, everyday life. As he soaked in steaming water, his resolve weakened and his mind filled with detailed pictures of Lacey, naked, covered in bubbles in the large bathtub on the other side of the wall.

He imagined her hair, wet, dark tendrils floating in the water. Then soaping herself, bubbles touching every inch of her creamy, delicate skin . . . think of nothing, he commanded himself.

Back in control, several delicious, thoughtless moments passed before Jared finally opened his eyes, more asleep than awake. The stars had come out and were brilliant against the pitch-dark sky. *No moon tonight.* He identified the stars and planets he knew, then his heavy-lidded eyes closed again.

He felt so relaxed, so comfortable.

What am I doing here? This is about the stupidest thing I've done in a long time. Jared's jaw clenched. Another picture of Lacey flashed into his mind. She was beautiful, that was no lie. And how did she make her hair so soft. So touchable. While posing for the photographs he'd hardly been able to resist plunging his hands into her dark auburn curls. He wanted to bury his face in it.

She's a career woman. And a successful one at that. Joann had been good enough to remind him of that. He didn't need that kind of complication, now or ever.

A nagging voice planted new words for him to consider. *Maybe it doesn't have to be serious. Who says every relationship has to be serious, anyway?*

He answered himself. *Why start something if it's going to end?* Reluctantly, he realized his groin had the best argument. Even in the hot water he was reacting just to the thought of her. He felt like a teenager sneaking peeks at his father's *Playboy. Fantasy woman.* Why go through with it if it's not real? He imagined them together, and the ache increased. It had been a long time. Too long? Reluctantly, he admitted that he missed the touch of a woman.

Her hair neatly coiled on top of her head, Lacey rested her neck on a folded towel on the edge of the tub. *This is heaven. My next house must have a bathtub.*

She played with the bubbles, palming them, building sculptures on the curve of her breasts. Relax, she commanded herself, slamming her eyes shut. It was hard to slow down. Her life was busy, just the way she liked it. Nothing to complain about.

Except a little loneliness. Her eyes blinked open. Pushing the thought away, she eased herself deeper into the water. *I like my life. Of course it would be nice to share some things with someone. And I will, on my terms. My choice.*

The little voice inside her asked, *So why are you here?* They could have easily chosen not to stay the night, she knew that. Jamie's flu provided the prefect excuse.

But neither of them had brought it up.

And their hostess wouldn't have known that Jared's daughter was almost over her flu and, in fact, had been up watching videos when he'd called to check on her after their meal.

So, why am I here? She closed her eyes to concentrate. The only word that she was able to grasp among the many slippery excuses was *curiosity.* Maybe she needed to consider Kandy's advice and just have a little fun. *It's the nineties. I'm over twenty-one. I take the pill. Why not?*

A sharp rap at the bathroom door sent her adrenalin pumping. She sat up in the tub so abruptly that a generous amount of water and bubbles slapped onto the floor.

"Lacey? It's me."

"Well, *that's* a relief."

"I . . . I need to come in for a second. I cut myself on a piece of glass in the hot tub."

She sat up straighter. "Is it bad? Are you bleeding?"

The door opened a crack and she slid back into the water up to her chin.

"Sorry, I really need to come in."

Lacey strategically positioned the dwindling bubbles as he pushed open the bathroom door. Jared's face was flushed, his eyes filled with apologies.

She stared at him, her lips apart in appreciation. She took an instant inventory: wonderfully hairy chest, well-developed chest muscles, flat stomach, farmer-tanned arms, more dark hair just above the too-small towel that was knotted at his slim waist.

She watched as he turned around to show her the steadily expanding bloodstain on the towel—a stain originating from his right cheek.

"Oh, my goodness! What happened to your—"

"I'm afraid you're going to have to help me bandage it or something. I don't think there's any glass in it or anything."

"Well, don't just stand there, hand me a towel, Jared."

He snatched a towel off the counter by the sink, backed up toward her, and dangled it behind him for her to grab.

She stood up and wrapped the oversized towel securely around herself, making sure the ends were tightly tucked. "Okay, I'm decent. Now, if you're sure there's no glass, you should put some pressure on it while I look for a first-aid kit."

Jared's eyes were wide as he stared at her, but then he obeyed, putting one hand on his right buttock.

Suddenly she felt dry-mouthed, and the bathroom felt much smaller. Jared took a step toward the door to give her more room at the medicine cabinet. "Antacids, aspirin, toothpaste, mouthwash . . ." As she continued her search, a box of condoms fell out of the cabinet into the sink.

Her cheeks flushed with sudden heat as she caught Jared's stare of amusement in the mirror.

"This *is* the honeymoon cabin, remember."

Lacey continued to stare at his reflection. His damp hair gave him a impish look, and a devilish expression came into his eyes. "Hush, or I'll start looking for something really painful like rubbing alcohol." She couldn't help smiling back.

"Let's check underneath." When she squatted to open the cabinet below the sink, her arm grazed his leg. "Sorry." This time Jared didn't step backward out of her way.

She looked up for an instant, and his eyes held her still. A sultry moment froze between them. Blinking hard, she turned her attention back to the cupboard. "Eureka! At last."

She pulled out a familiar-looking blue and white plastic first-aid kit and opened its lid. "Gauze, tape, scissors, scalpel—just kidding."

"Right." A huskiness lingered in his tone.

She licked her lips. "You're going to have to, uh, move the towel so I can see exactly what I need. How big a bandage you need."

"Be gentle," he teased, obediently turning his back to her. Deftly he undid his towel and flipped it to cover his front.

Lacey occupied herself, laying out antiseptic wipes

and different sized bandage strips. When she was ready she directed her gaze to Jared's right cheek. The wound was still bleeding a little, but it was small.

"Well?" he asked.

"Looks deep, but not that bad. This is going to sting a little." She watched his muscles tense only slightly as she rubbed the blood off his skin with an antiseptic wipe.

Jared turned his head, stretching his neck to try to see her handiwork. With one eyebrow raised he asked, "Will I have a scar?"

She flashed him a good-natured smile. "Hope so. Just think of it as a souvenir."

"Not one I can share with too many people."

She blushed at his remark, the fact that she was staring at his behind becoming just a little too real. "This is just a little antibiotic cream. It shouldn't hurt," she said, dabbing the cream on the wound. She finished with a bandage square. "All done."

"You sound like Jamie." Jared readjusted his towel and turned to face her. "Thanks, Lacey. You have a gentle touch."

She impulsively brought her hand to the front of her towel to secure it. Frozen again, she watched as he bent toward her. Her gaze locked on his full lips as they slowly descended to meet hers.

At the last moment, his head turned so that his lips touched her cheek. He lingered there for just a moment, then pulled back.

Shivers of delight followed his touch. She searched his eyes and saw a smile there that contained a sensuous flame.

"Are you done?" he asked.

"What?"

"With your bath. The water's probably cold."

"Oh. Right."

"You hungry?"

She nodded.

"How 'bout we both get dressed and I'll check out the snacks in the fridge. We could eat out on the deck."

"Sounds great." She watched him turn and quietly close the door behind him.

There was a tingling in the pit of her stomach and her thoughts spun. *Okay, it was just a kiss on the cheek. Nothing more.*

The mirror above the sink betrayed her emotions as she stared at herself. Reddened cheeks, dilated pupils, the sheen of nervous perspiration on her upper lip.

Grabbing her makeup bag, she decided to forego her usual routine; she simply powdered her face and added a touch of lip gloss. Then she brushed her hair until it gleamed, the waves cascading down her back.

She slipped into clean panties and felt a slickness between her legs that confirmed her arousal. She closed her eyes, breathing deeply.

A soft knock at the door interrupted her meditation.

"Lacey?"

"I'm almost dressed. Be out in a second."

"I put the food out on the deck." His voice was low and smooth.

"Okay." She realized that the pounding of her own quickened heartbeat was competing with the fading thud of his footsteps. Irritated, she quickly pulled on jeans and a bright pink sweatshirt, then looked down at the slogan emblazoned on the front.

"Great," she said, reading *Hairdressers Do It With Style.*

ELEVEN

Much to Jared's delight, the contest sponsors had loaded the cabin's tiny refrigerator with gourmet delicacies: jumbo boiled shrimp, artichoke hearts, an assortment of sliced cheese, a small fruit and vegetable platter, caviar, pate, and hand-dipped chocolate truffles.

Waiting for Lacey, Jared had rummaged in the cupboards and discovered napkins, paper plates and bowls, a box of crackers, and plastic champagne glasses.

He busied himself putting a little bit of everything on plates, running back and forth to the deck. On his final trip, he brought out one of the three bottles of champagne that were also in the refrigerator, each bearing a gift tag from businesses that had sponsored the bachelor auction.

He had changed into faded jeans and a long-sleeved denim shirt. The night was beginning to feel cooler already. Maybe he'd have to build a fire after all, he thought.

As he popped the top off the champagne, Jared looked up to see Lacey stepping onto the deck. The first thing he noticed was her hair, free-flowing and sexy as hell. His gaze roamed over her figure, ending at her feet—bare, with bright red polished toenails.

"Wow, was all that in that little fridge? It looks great," she said.

"I wasn't sure what you liked, so I took a little of everything."

He stared as she walked to one of the chairs and sat down. Suddenly he felt ravenous.

"I don't know about you, but I'm starved," she said, dipping one of the shrimp into cocktail sauce.

He watched as she bit into it, staring, really, as the tip of her tongue found a bit of sauce on her upper lip.

"I see you found the champagne."

He nodded.

"Aren't you going to have anything?"

Jared blinked, trying to clear his head. He sat down and unconsciously began to fill a plate.

After a few minutes of silence, Lacey poured the champagne and held out a glass to him.

"I hope you're good at toasts," she said.

Was he imagining her warm green eyes were filled with expectation? His gaze dropped to stare at the bubbles in his glass, then returned to once again rest on her luminous emerald eyes.

He cleared his throat. "Well, I guess you're just supposed to say what's on your mind—"

"Or in your heart," she finished.

"Right. Well, here's to us." He paused, thinking. "And I'm kind of glad the way things turned out. You're probably a much better date than my sister."

Lacey's eyes widened a little. "I'll take that as a compliment—though I wouldn't tell your sister, if I were you."

He returned her grin and touched the rim of her glass with his. He took a long draw of champagne and watched as she drained half of hers in a series of swallows.

Both returned their attention to the food, stopping

periodically to refill their glasses until the bottle was empty.

Lacey leaned back in her chair, her hands resting on her stomach.

"You warm enough out here?" he asked.

She rubbed her bare feet together. "It's just now starting to feel cool to me. Why don't you build a fire and I'll clean up out here."

Jared stood, avoiding her gaze. Lacey by firelight might just be the death of me, he thought.

Standing in the kitchenette, Lacey snuck a peek at Jared while he placed several small logs in the fireplace. Her fingers trembled as she tucked clear wrap over the leftovers from their picnic. Three glasses of champagne had created a delicious buzz. She felt relaxed. Feminine. She felt everything. She could feel that her nipples were tight as they brushed against the soft fabric inside her sweatshirt. Her panties felt damp. She tingled from head to toe.

"You ready?" Jared called.

She smiled at the double meaning of his innocent question. Her intense desire was an unexpected surprise. Looking up, she checked his progress. *Do you feel the same?* Suddenly her mouth went dry. What if he didn't?

Turning away, Lacey gripped the edge of the counter until her knuckles drained of blood. *Don't be a fool. A little control right now is what you need, not wanton lust.*

Jared sat cross-legged in front of the fire and didn't move when she approached. She joined him on the sheepskin rug. Several minutes passed wordlessly.

"It's a nice fire," she murmured.

Jared tilted his head toward her, catching her gaze. "How do you feel?"

"About what?"

"Us. Being here. Tonight."

Lacey didn't answer. Instead, she tore her gaze from his and stared at the fire, watching the flames curl around a log, softly, almost lovingly.

"Should I get us some more champagne?" he asked.

She hesitated before answering. "I'd like that."

Jared gracefully got to his feet and occupied himself in the tiny kitchen.

She knew more champagne would weaken her resolve. *But maybe that's exactly what I need. Just have a little fun. Everyone else does it.* A tiny voice inside her head laughed at her feeble attempt at justification.

Jared returned and placed a bottle and glasses on the floor in front of her. "Look, let's just relax. Talk. I promise to be a gentleman, scout's honor."

Lacey smiled, relieved at his humor. She glanced at him and saw his three fingers frozen in a scout's pledge. "Deal."

Jared wiped imaginary sweat from his forehead, then lowered his hand. Returning her smile, he felt immediately more relaxed. He filled their glasses. This time they drank without a toast. Was he just imagining the flare of desire in her eyes?

Their silence was strangely comfortable. He considered his own past—dates before Marsha, after Marsha, other times he'd been alone with women. He was surprised at the ease he felt sitting in silence with Lacey.

Maybe she *was* different. Maybe he needed to rethink his rules. What did he know? She was successful, but not arrogant about it. She seemed awfully young, but she was great with Jamie. Remembering Hank, she didn't appear to have the best judgment in men, but on the other hand, she was willing to admit her mistakes.

He needed to know more about her.

"Penny for your thoughts?" Lacey said softly.

"Truth?"

"Oh, this sounds like the beginning of twenty questions—"

"Afraid?" Her silence told him she was, but he continued anyway. "Well, how else can we get to know each other?"

"Okay, let's set the ground rules. We get to ask what we want, but we each retain the right to say 'pass.' " She refilled her glass and met his stare.

"Fair enough. Who starts?" he asked.

"I offered the penny."

He drained his glass and refilled it before he answered, settling back, cross-legged on the floor. "Well, actually, I was wondering if you were different from other women, or if I was just imagining it."

"Please phrase your answer in the form of a question." Her silky voice held a challenge.

He stared at her profile, raising one eyebrow, and asked what he really wanted to know. "How important is your career to you?"

Lacey kept her gaze on the curling flames of the fire. "Interesting question. My career is probably one of the few things I've done right in my life. I'm good at it. I can support myself. I'm up for a promotion. It's fulfilling to me."

Jared winced slightly. "So you enjoy working all the time?"

She paused. "I'm working on slowing down, actually. The girls call me a workaholic. I think I'm ready for . . . a hobby, maybe."

Well, now I'm confused. Jared added his gaze to the flames.

She interrupted his thoughts. "You have something against women with careers?"

Uh-oh. "It depends."

"On?"

Jared caught her gaze. She looked so innocent, so open.

"Looks like I touched a nerve. You can pass if you want," she offered.

He took a deep breath and returned his gaze to the fire. "Jamie's mom chose her career over . . . us."

They sat in thick silence for several moments.

"Do you want to talk about it? About her?" Lacey asked.

Jared's mind filled with all the painful memories he'd worked so hard to suppress. Would she understand? Or would she take Marsha's side?

He rotated his shoulders, trying to release the tension that had instantly developed. "I've loved having Jamie to myself. I never thought Marsha—that's Jamie's mom—really wanted a kid. She just kind of . . . did it, you know?"

"I know women like that," she said.

"And I still can't understand how she could just leave us for a career, choose her job instead of her family." His jaw clenched tightly as he closed his eyes against the flood of emotion he was experiencing.

"Some women shouldn't have children," she began, "and you have to remember that Jamie's lucky she's got a dad like you. It's just going to be hard, sometimes, to handle the girl stuff. Your sister will be a big help."

"She is," he agreed, "when she's around. She gets busy, though, and I can't go running to her with every little problem."

"You know what? It's going to be quite a while before it feels like there're problems you can't handle."

He looked at her. It wasn't the conversation he'd expected. Maybe she *was* different.

She flashed a smile. "We did pretty well, don't you think?"

"My turn. I heard you were engaged, but it didn't work out. What happened?"

This time, it was Lacey who turned away. Her cheeks flushed hot and her stomach tied itself into a neat little knot. "Well, you certainly cut to the chase."

"Need to pass?" he asked.

It sounded more like a dare to her than an offering.

Why not? It felt good to talk, to share.

"Lacey?"

"I was engaged to the wrong man."

"What was wrong?"

"Everything. In a nutshell, I was a trusting female and he was a philandering jerk."

"Details?"

"Okay." She took in a deep breath and continued. "He was eight years older than me. He had an adorable little boy named Sean. He fooled around with his secretary, she got pregnant, and he left town with her, taking Sean out of my life. That was about a year ago."

Son of a bitch. Gloria was right about her broken heart.

"Anyone since?" he asked.

"Celibacy is in, haven't you heard?" She paused before adding, "Neither one of us sounds too successful in the love department." Her voice was quiet, serene.

Jared felt her hand, whisper soft on his knee. He looked down at it, tiny and pale on his jeans. He looked into her eyes. They danced with green fire. He wondered if she knew how pretty she was.

Keeping her gaze, Jared placed his hand on top of hers and gently squeezed it. He watched her eyes widen and glimmer with unasked questions.

He leaned toward her. She was so beautiful. Her dark auburn hair cascaded over her shoulders, shimmering with lights reflected from the fire. "I want to kiss you." He waited for a response.

He watched as Lacey leaned toward him, her gaze never wavering.

Jared brought his hand up to cup her chin. Her skin felt like silk. As he held her gaze he stroked her bottom lip with the pad of his thumb. Her eyes closed at his touch.

Time slowed as his pulse quickened. His fingers ached to touch her. Soon his other hand was lost in her hair as he drew her closer to him.

He softly kissed the corner of her mouth, gently bringing the tip of his tongue to her skin for a taste. He breathed in her fruity, musky scent. Her nearness was overwhelming.

He heard a soft moan and wondered if the sound came from his own throat or hers. His hand dropped to her throat and he felt her pulse beat, accelerating at his caress.

"Kiss me," she whispered.

TWELVE

Their lips melted together in a lingering, delicious moment. A long, gentle kiss. Unhurried. Purposeful. Lacey groaned softly when Jared pulled his mouth from hers; and again when his tongue traced her lips.

She needed more.

Her fingers cupped the nape of his neck, tugging him toward her. Their lips met again and she felt his arms wrap around her; so strong, so right. Her fingers buried themselves in his hair.

This time the kiss was deeper. Their tongues shared an intimate dance until she moaned and pulled away for air. His kiss was intoxicating.

She stared into his stormy gray eyes, eyes she wanted to get lost in. Her emotions whirled and skidded dangerously out of control.

"You okay?" he whispered.

She nodded. They were both adults, she told herself. *Consenting adults.*

"Do you want me to stop?" A huskiness lingered in his tone.

Did she? In a split second she rationalized that whatever was going to happen between them was theirs alone. No one gets hurt. No one else's business.

"Lacey?"

There was an invitation in the smoldering depths of his eyes and in his low, silvery voice. She took a frank, admiring look at him, studying his face feature by feature. His skin was weathered from the sun and wind, a slight pinkness on his strong nose. Laugh lines at the corners of his eyes betrayed his humor and softened his expression.

Lacey raised both hands to touch him, her fingertips tracing his eyebrows, then dropping to caress a path down his cheeks.

When her fingertips touched his lips, his eyes closed. She could feel his breath against her face, whisper soft. She drank in his sweet fragrance, the scent of his desire added to the mix of champagne and the familiar smell of apricots.

A low, tormented sound escaped from Jared's throat as she felt his hands at the small of her back. In one smooth movement he drew her against him, their lips fusing sweetly in a devouring kiss.

She felt both his hands slide under her shirt, stroking her skin, massaging her back. His touch sent currents of desire through her as he deepened the kiss. She felt transported, her thoughts spinning, a quiver of titillation raging through her. It had never been like this for her. This was raw. This was real. She felt helpless to resist.

As their bodies sank to the floor, Jared pulled her so that she lay on top of him. With a moan, she pulled her lips away and stared into his stormy eyes. She searched for clues there. *What was he thinking?* She felt his hands move under her shirt, finding the curve of her breasts with his thumbs.

"No bra," he declared, surprise in his voice.

She lifted her chest from his to encourage his sensual exploration. Dizzy with longing, she repositioned her hands on the floor, one on each side of his shoulders. As her fingers sank into the softness of the sheepskin rug, she lifted her torso, allowing him less of a barrier.

As his hands cupped her breasts, he tenderly squeezed and rubbed her nipples between his finger and thumb. Lacey gasped as a tingle surged from her nipple to the moistness between her thighs. She watched the bright flare of desire spring into Jared's eyes. *He wanted her.*

"So soft," he whispered as he rubbed and lightly pinched. "I want to see you," he said as he tugged at her sweatshirt. She helped him pull the shirt over her head, her hair spilling against his chest.

Lacey tossed the shirt out of the way and sat up, straddling Jared's hips. She watched his eyes darken with arousal as he stared at her breasts. She was surprised how easily she had bared herself to him.

With trembling fingers she reached for the buttons of his shirt. She wanted like mad to feel her skin against his. He tugged his shirt out of his jeans, and started unbuttoning from the bottom, meeting her in the middle. Then he lifted his shoulders off the rug to make it easier for her to remove the shirt.

Lacey remained upright, running her hands over his chest.

"You make me crazy," he said.

"I want to."

With a deep moan, his hands reached for the top of her jeans, deftly unbuttoning them and drawing the zipper down as far as he could. She felt his fingers slip under the top of her panties.

"Oh—" Her skin prickled with the heat of his touch.

"You want me to stop?" he asked, pausing in his exploration.

She should say yes; she knew that. Instead, she welcomed the heat that rippled under her skin, recognizing the flush of sexual desire, something she hadn't felt for a long, long time.

Without answering, Lacey tugged at Jared's jeans, struggling with the buttons under the fly. His large hands covered hers, calming her struggle.

"Why don't we take a minute and get . . . comfortable."

She smiled at his composure in the heat of the moment, grateful for his gentlemanly manner. She gasped as his hands once again cupped her breasts, as though he needed to touch them before they moved from their intimate position.

Lacey eased herself off him and they each slipped out of their jeans. She shivered, suddenly feeling chilly and a little awkward, the spell interrupted by their need to get out of their clothes. She sat, knees to her chin, facing the warmth of the fire.

"Do you know how beautiful you are?" She felt his hands slip under her hair, massaging her shoulders, instantly locating the spot where her tension always accumulated.

"Magic hands," she murmured.

Jared continued to methodically knead the soft flesh of Lacey's shoulders until he felt her muscles relax, her posture soften. He leaned his face closer to her hair, finally touching his cheek to it. He'd wanted to bury himself in her silky mane since the moment he'd met her.

His body ached to touch her. He sucked in his cheeks, biting them to distract himself, prevent himself from hurrying things. *Go slow. Go slow.*

He needed to be sure, sure that Lacey wanted this as much as he did. He hoped like hell she did. This was different. This wasn't a quick roll in the hay just because it was convenient.

Gratefully, he felt his erection soften slightly as he massaged and stroked her skin. He knew a mere kiss would once again set his body aflame. He wanted to linger over her, take his time with her.

His hands left her shoulders and he scooted closer, pulling her against him so her back rested against his chest, his legs stretched out on either side of her, sinking into the soft sheepskin.

The quiet between them felt troubled. He sensed her shyness. He reminded himself that it had been a while between lovers for her too.

Finally he felt her body relax against him and he wrapped his arms around her in an intimate hug. Relaxing his hold on her, he began to rub her knees, then her shins and calves. Soon he felt her head tilt back to rest under his chin.

"You sure know how to build a fire," she said, her voice sounding dreamy and calm.

"You too." He wondered if she knew how hot she'd made him. With her straddling his erection and his hands on her breasts, he'd felt like he would explode. He felt like a teenager, all hormones and no sense.

Running his hands up her leg, he nudged her thighs and Lacy dropped her legs. He felt her sigh against him and his hands moved to hold her breasts. Drawing circles around her nipples with his finger, he felt himself reharden instantly. He shifted his position, freeing his erection so that it lay against the small of her back.

He felt her stiffen. "No hurry," he whispered. "I'm fine. I just want to touch you."

Relieved at his words, Lacey snuggled against Jared's chest, her self-consciousness replaced by the delicious pleasure of his touch. The warmth from the fire against her bare skin competed with the inner flame, increasing with his tender caresses.

She stared at the flames as his fingers gently squeezed and stroked both nipples, drawing them to pebble hardness. An uncontrollable groan escaped her lips as he freed one breast to sear a path down her abdomen and onto her thigh. He paused, as if waiting for reassurance.

Shifting so she sat closer against him, Lacey moved her leg so Jared's fingers came to rest between her thighs. *Yes. Yes.* It had been a long time. Blake had been an acceptable lover, but tended to be more of a slam-bam-thank-you-ma'am kind of guy. Short on foreplay, long on sleeping the night away.

Jared slowly stretched his fingers, caressing her mound. She felt the thud of his heart quicken against her back. They were so close together she wasn't sure she could feel where his body ended and hers began. Gently, he stroked her inner folds, his fingers quickly becoming slick.

"You're so wet, so hot," he whispered in her ear. His voice broke with huskiness.

The intimacy of his touch blocked Lacey's ability to speak. All she could think about was how good it felt, how good she felt with his hands on her. She gasped sharply when he found her clitoris. After a moment's pause, he began a sensual massage of slow, steady circles.

Waves of ecstasy rippled through her as his fingers magically brought her to the peak of desire, then paused just long enough to prevent her climax. How did he know that half the pleasure was in the journey? His slow, soft touch was new to her. It was as though his hands knew exactly where to touch her.

"Jared," she whispered.

"Mmm?"

"I want to feel you . . . inside me." Lacey stopped the movement of his hands and turned to face him. Her entire body tingled with delicious desire. She stared at him, watching the firelight that glittered in his gray eyes. His breathing became heavy and ragged.

"You are so beautiful," he whispered, touching her breasts, using the slickness on his fingers to massage her taut nipples. When he heard her moan softly, he moved his hands to her waist and pulled her to him. He kissed her, lingering, savoring every movement of her velvet lips.

Lost in the kiss, he felt Lacey's hands on his shoulders, gently pushing him away. With a groan, he pulled his lips from hers, his mouth burning with fire.

God, she was gorgeous. Her cheeks were flushed, her emerald eyes wild, her hair sexily mussed. "Should I get a condom?" he asked softly.

She shook her head. "I'm on the pill. And after Blake left, I had two AIDS tests. I don't have anything else."

"Me, too. And I haven't been with anyone since Marsha. You sure you want to . . . ?"

Lacey put her fingers to his lips to quiet his question. She nodded her reply and pulled him toward her. They fell softly to the floor together. She gasped as bare chest met bare chest. With the softness of the sheepskin against her back, she wiggled her hips, adjusting her position beneath him. She felt his hardness between her legs. He didn't move. He was waiting for her, waiting for direction. *Amazing.*

Staring into Jared's eyes, Lacey watched the play of emotions on his face. His gray eyes darkened with desire as she held his gaze. He waited a moment more, then captured her mouth with a devouring kiss.

She felt his hardness nudging between her legs. Still he waited for her approval. Sliding her hand between their bodies, she grasped his shaft, squeezing and stroking. A low groan rumbled in Jared's throat, then his lips left hers.

"You're killing me."

Smiling wickedly, she shifted her hips, then guided his shaft to her hot, moist entrance.

His eyes widened and flamed with desire. As he thrust inside her, she gasped at his ability to completely fill her, unconsciously squeezing him, drawing him in more deeply.

"You're so tight, so wet," he whispered. "So good."

Heat raced through her as she closed her eyes, her head spinning. It felt dangerous. It felt wonderful.

Her skin goosebumped as she rocked against him, riding wave after wave of ecstasy. *So close. So close.* Her fingers dug into Jared's back as she pulled him closer, closer.

She wanted him deeper. Closer. Tilting her pelvis and rocking against him, she heard Jared's moan. She opened her eyes to watch him.

"I can't wait much longer," he said. "You feel too good."

"Don't wait."

She encouraged his thrusts to go deeper, faster, until the spiraling force of her own climax engulfed her. Stars exploded and she felt strangely detached from her body; at the same time, connected intimately to every cell. She shuddered.

"Oh, Jared . . ." Her voice was a breathless whimper.

As soon as her spasms had quieted, Jared felt his own spiral building. He felt her intimate grasp as he sunk deeper and deeper into her. Surprise flashed in her eyes as he stared into their emerald depths.

They moved together so well, so smoothly, their bodies in exquisite harmony. The hot tide of passion raged between them as they clung to each other, both soaring over the edge together.

THIRTEEN

In the middle of the night Jared woke. *It hadn't been a dream.* Lacey was still snuggled next to him, their legs entwined, her silky hair draped over his chest. He felt her shiver. The fire had burned down to white hot embers and the room was getting chilly.

"Lacey," he whispered. Gently, he stroked her hair until she stirred. A sleepy smile came to her lips, and he leaned toward her to kiss them.

He felt himself stiffen in response; instantly ready, embarrassed at the effect she had on him. "Hi, there, sleepyhead."

"Who's sleepy?" she asked, her eyes still half-closed.

"What do you say about moving to the bed? This floor is getting harder by the moment and my back isn't what it used to be."

Lacey nodded and let him help her to her feet. The thought of slipping between the crisp linen sheets of the four-poster was almost too delicious. *A girl could get used to this.* As soon as the thought formed, she squelched it. It was only one night, she reminded herself. Tomorrow everything would return to normal.

"I'm going to duck in here for a minute," Jared said as he left her in the hall and stepped into the bathroom.

She walked quickly into the bedroom. Jared was absolutely not the kind of man she needed in her life right now—or ever, she thought. Too many things going against it. Besides, he'd already told her he didn't understand career women. And then there was Jamie. Too complicated. Her heart couldn't take another wound. *End it before it begins.*

She pulled back the covers and crawled into the bed, sinking into a layer of softness that almost made her swoon. There was a thick, downy featherbed between the fitted sheet and mattress. Luxuriously cozy. Obscenely soft. She cuddled under the covers.

Staring at the ceiling, she wondered if she should put something on. *Like what?* The girls had conveniently taken out her pajamas. Wearing the white negligee was not the message she should be sending. Frowning, she rationalized what had happened. *Making love in front of the fire—two lonely adults, too much champagne, weakened resolve.*

Flinging the covers back, she stepped out of the bed and grabbed an oversized T-shirt and clean panties. Just as she heard the sound of the bathroom door, she slipped back into the bed, pulled the covers to her chest, and turned her face away from the door.

Eyes closed, she strained to hear the sound of Jared's footsteps. Either he was awfully light on his feet or maybe he'd gone somewhere else. When she felt his weight sink the opposite edge of the bed, it startled her enough to make her gasp.

"You okay?" he asked.

"Just tired. Goodnight, Jared. See you in the morning."

Lacey waited, listening to the heavy silence until she fell into a troubled sleep.

Jared's jaw clenched tightly as he sat on the edge of the bed. He stared into the darkness until he heard Lacey's slow, even breathing, then turned to look at her.

I don't get it. A couple of short hours ago they had been more intimate than he'd ever allowed himself to be with any of the women in his life. Now she was sound asleep, as though nothing had happened between them.

He shook his head. Maybe he was wrong after all. The thought sickened him. How could he have been fooled like that? He had even begun to think they might be falling in love. *I'm an idiot.*

In her sleep, Lacey rolled toward him, her hair covering half her face. Carefully he reached out to take a lock of her hair, leaning forward so he could bring it to his cheek. *So soft, finer than silk.* As he brought it to his lips he remembered how it had felt draped over his chest. He frowned. It had felt so *right* to be with her. How could he be so wrong?

In the starlight, she looked like an angel. He stared at her for several minutes, wanting to remember everything about her.

Murmuring in her sleep as though she was having a bad dream, Lacey tossed and turned in the big bed. Jared brushed her cheek with the back of his hand and whispered soothing words, just like he had done hundreds of times for Jamie.

He watched her face. Soon her furrowed brow was

replaced by a soft smile. He leaned closer to her and kissed her forehead. When he pulled away from her, her eyes half opened and she raised her hand as if to touch him. Sleep overtook her and she snuggled deeper under the covers.

Jared sighed and stood up. Might as well see how comfortable the sofa is, he thought, knowing he wouldn't be able to get any sleep at all lying next to her.

His body ached for her. Looking at her, he felt his heart ache as well.

A soft knocking at the cabin door stirred Lacey from her dream. Keeping her eyes closed, she tried to recapture its essence. *Jared.* Something about walking . . . Jamie between them holding their hands . . . the smell of apricots . . . a well-worn path . . . stopping to pick flowers, stealing a kiss . . .

Lacey's eyes flew open. Her gaze darted around the room and, in an instant, she remembered where she was, what had happened. Her body reacted to the memory with a throbbing tingle between her thighs. Just the thought of him sent her pulse racing.

Closing her eyes and sinking her head into the pillow, she scolded herself. *Dreams are one thing, but this is not going any further.*

The sound of the front door opening and closing got her attention. She looked up to see Jared's face at the bedroom door.

"Good morning." His voice was neutral.

"Was that our breakfast arriving?" she asked, pushing herself up on both elbows.

"Yup. Smells good. I've already showered. If you want, I'll set up outside and you can clean up."

"Meet you on the patio in about fifteen minutes," she answered, grateful for the time to get her thoughts collected.

She watched Jared disappear from sight, then climbed out of the bed, gathering clean clothes and her toiletries. She knew a quick shower would help clear her head. And she would need a clear head if she was going to share breakfast with the man she had made love to the night before.

They ate silently, occasionally sharing thoughts about how flaky the croissants were, how fresh the peaches seemed. Two cups of coffee later and the silence felt more comfortable.

Lacey spoke first. "I wonder what time check-out is."

"There's a flyer taped inside the cupboard in the kitchen. Three o'clock."

"Oh." No other words came to her. After their intimacy, she was amazed at how intermittently awkward she felt. She stared past Jared and searched for words.

"Did you want to stay? We could go for a walk or . . ." His voiced drifted off, not finishing the sentence.

"I guess I hadn't thought that far," she said. Her stomach tightened. "I figured you might want to get back early to check on Jamie. I didn't know if your animals needed care or . . ."

Jared stared at her. It was like she was a different person in the light of day. He wished like hell he could turn back the clock, be with the Lacey he had been with the night before.

"I was thinking," she began, "that if you wanted

to get back, I could give Kandy a call and ask her to come get me, go to lunch and do some shopping on the way home."

"Sounds fine. I should get back to the ranch." *It sounded awful.* It was as though she couldn't wait to be apart from him. He felt a painful tug on his heart. Maybe she just needed some time. Time to think.

"Okay, it's a plan," she said.

Her voice sounded overly cheerful to him. Something was wrong, but it was obvious that last night meant more to him than it did to her. *Fine.* He didn't need the aggravation.

"I'll clean up," she offered, gathering the breakfast dishes.

Jared didn't answer her, instead he left her on the patio and busied himself in the cabin, packing his small leather bag. When he was finished, he placed it near the front door, leaning his guitar case against the wall.

Lacey looked up from the kitchenette. "I didn't get to hear you play your guitar," she said, a hint of disappointment in her voice.

Jared replied without looking at her. "Maybe some other time."

Lacey didn't answer. *Some other time?* She brought her fingers to her temples, trying to rub away the headache that was developing. *A champagne headache.*

When Lacey looked up, Jared was standing on the other side of the counter.

"You okay?" he asked.

"Just a little headache. I'm fine."

"I was thinking of going for a walk. I promised Jamie I'd bring her one of those giant pinecones for her collection. Maybe the air would help your head," he suggested.

Lacey nodded. *Perhaps it would.* She followed him to the door.

Jared reached for the doorknob and held the door open. When Lacey passed through he followed close behind her, impulsively reaching for a curl. What was it about her hair that drove him crazy, he wondered. Shaking his head, he stepped forward so they walked side by side.

"There's a path over here. I saw it yesterday." Jared pointed to the side of the cabin.

"It's so pretty here. So peaceful. You sure you don't mind me taking advantage of the rest of the day?" she asked.

"Nope. Enjoy." And he meant it. If things had turned out differently, he thought, they would have spent the day making love, soaking in the hot tub, and napping in the luxury of the four-poster. He sighed. He wished things had turned out differently.

"Here's one," Lacey said, stooping to pick up a pinecone the size of a pineapple. "Coulter pine, right?"

"Right." Jared smiled. At least she had been paying attention on the ride up.

"Look," she said, pointing at a trailhead sign. "Manzanita Trail: two point five miles."

Jared looked skeptically at her thin-soled sandals and gauze skirt. She was dressed more for a day of shopping than for a hike, even on an easy trail.

Hands on her hips, Lacey declared, "The air seems to be helping my headache. Do you mind if I go on ahead?"

"I should be getting back, anyway."

Lacey took a deep breath.

Jared took the pinecone out of her hands. "Well . . ."

"Thanks for everything. It was a nice evening." Lacey finished his thought and looked away, staring down the trail, seemingly eager for the conversation to end.

"Sure." Jared tossed the pinecone from hand to hand. He didn't feel right leaving her in the woods. *She's a grown woman. She should be able to take care of herself.*

He forced his voice to sound cheerful. "See you around." He pivoted and strode away from her. Maybe it was for the best, he thought.

Lacey watched Jared's figure until he disappeared from view around a bend in the path. Too bad, she thought. Too bad our situations aren't different.

She would miss his company, she realized, already wishing he was walking beside her as she started down the trail. She would miss him telling her about the bushes and trees and flowers along the trail. *He's everything you aren't looking for,* she reminded herself.

Concentrating on her footing as she walked, Lacey pushed away all the thoughts and feelings that had anything to do with Jared. Instead, she listened to the sound of the wind as it swished through the leaves of the trees, pausing at mysterious rustling sounds in the underbrush, hoping to see some wildlife.

The piercing cry of a hawk grabbed Lacey's attention. She shaded her eyes as she peered into the treetops, searching for the bird. A shadow streaked past as she took a step forward.

"Where *are* you?" she muttered as she took another step forward—forward into air instead of the uneven stony trail. She hadn't noticed that the pathway had fallen away, forcing a large step downward onto a slab of granite.

As Lacey tumbled out of control, she yelped in surprise, falling heavily onto one knee. Stabs of pain shot through her ankle as starbursts exploded behind her eyelids.

FOURTEEN

Jared made quick time between Lacey and the cabin. His jaws ached with the tension he felt.

Damn. Why was it so hard to just stop thinking about her?

He entered the cabin and walked to the fireplace, putting the treasured pinecone on the mantel. He closed his eyes and rotated his neck, the restless night on the lumpy couch beginning to catch up with him. Suddenly forty-three felt older than he was willing to admit. *Damn.*

He stirred the fireplace, checking for signs of burning coals, then walked slowly through each room. It was a nice place, he thought. He allowed a few dangerous memories to seep into his thoughts; the hot tub, her gentle care of his wound, her eyes by firelight, the feel of her silky hair against his cheek. Pausing in the kitchenette, Jared stared toward the fireplace, his gaze stopping at the sheepskin rug.

He had felt powerless against the passion he'd felt for her. His pulse quickened, remembering the feel of her skin against his, her fragrance, the taste of her, how her soft curves molded to his body.

And her lips. Their kisses had left his mouth burning with fire. The velvet warmth of her total response to him was amazing. They were good together.

Forget about her, he commanded himself, angrily

turning away from the scene of the previous night's passion. Jaws clenched, Jared grabbed his leather tote and stormed out of the cabin.

Lacey scooted herself off the rocky trail so she was sitting, instead, on a soft bed of pine needles. Her ankle had swollen to twice its normal size, black and blue shades developing quickly.

Gingerly she touched the growing lump, wincing at the pain that followed. Her eyes filled with tears of frustration, knowing the fall wouldn't have happened if Jared had been along. He would have warned her of the sudden drop in the trail, and she would have taken his arm for support when she'd felt her feet slip on loose stones.

Jared.

A loud fluttering in the tree forced her to look away from her injured ankle. Directly above was the elusive hawk that had distracted her.

"*Now* you show up," she grumbled. "Where were you when my feet were firmly planted on the ground?"

The hawk tilted its head at the sound of her voice. "Cack-cack-cack."

Startled at the bird's cry, Lacey took a quick, sharp breath. "Calm down—*I'm* the one in trouble here." She stared at the bird, squinting, trying to see it more clearly. "You're quite handsome, aren't you? Almost *worth* twisting my ankle over."

The bird continued to stare at her.

Lacey leaned back on her hands, elevating her foot on a nearby boulder, hoping to lessen the painful throbbing. It was a beautiful bird, brown and white breast feathers, slate blue wings.

"Cack-cack-cack."

"Take it easy," Lacey murmured. "You wouldn't feel like flying down the mountain and sending a certain cowboy in a pickup truck back to rescue me, would you?"

"Cack-cack-cack."

"Didn't think so," she whispered, closing her eyes at a sudden jab of pain.

A tear threatened to escape from behind her tightly closed eyes, and her throat ached with the undeniable feeling of defeat. She should have asked him to walk with her. It was that simple. His eyes had betrayed his disappointment and she had chosen to ignore it.

The knowledge of her regret twisted and turned inside her. He was a nice guy. *But not for me.* And it certainly wasn't fair to lead him on, she thought. Their night together had been a mistake—a wonderful mistake, she admitted, but still a mistake. It had happened, and now it was over.

She sighed heavily, and a flash of loneliness stabbed at her. *Jared.* She already missed him, missed his touch.

"Cack-cack-cack."

She opened her eyes and saw the hawk fly away. *Well, let's hope someone comes down this trail to rescue me.*

Almost an hour into the drive home, Jared slapped the steering wheel with the palm of his hand. *Shoot.* In his angry haste to leave the cabin, he'd left Jamie's pinecone on the mantel *and* forgotten his guitar.

He'd have to go back. He slowed, turned the pickup around, and headed back to the cabin.

Would she be there? He couldn't help wondering,

hoping. Maybe she'd be back from her walk and they could clear the troubled air between them. He hated how he felt. Too many unanswered questions.

Sure, she was young, he thought. *And a career woman,* he reminded himself. In fact, she'd made it crystal clear that her career was the most important thing in her life.

Just like Marsha. And he certainly didn't need to learn that lesson again. His marriage had been a series of too many disappointments, too many arguments. The only bright moment had been Jamie. Career women were alike, he maintained. Serious about their promotions, the bottom line, and how to squeeze as much money from the public as possible.

Forget her.

Jared turned into the driveway of the bed and breakfast and parked. As he neared the cabin he noticed a note tacked to the door, fluttering in the breeze.

Mr. Conrad: the Ranger took your lady friend down the mountain to Urgent Care. She said to leave a note that you might be back for your guitar. We have it up at the house along with the rest of the things—Mrs. Miller.

His heart in his throat, Jared immediately considered the worst-case scenario. Mountain lion. *I shouldn't have left her alone on the trail.* Swearing, he tore the note from the door and ran toward the main house.

As Jared flung open the kitchen door, he saw Mrs. Miller was on the phone, gesturing for him to take the receiver. "It's the doctor. Here, you talk to him."

"Mr. Conrad?"

"Is she all right? What happened?" Fear and anger knotted painfully inside him. The muscles of his forearm hardened beneath his sleeve as he held the receiver in a death grip.

"Just a bad sprain," the voice replied. "Right ankle. She'll need to keep off her feet for a couple days. No hiking for a while. A friend came to take her home."

A war of emotions raged within him—exasperation, relief, worry. *Why did he care so much?*

FIFTEEN

Jared parked his truck at the curb in front of Lacey's house. He stared at the beautifully manicured lawn, a sea of green, each blade identical in height; the delicate flowers that bordered its front, patches of pink and fuschia; old-fashioned lace curtains at every window. The little house looked like Lacey.

What would he say to her? Suddenly he wasn't precisely sure what he wanted to accomplish. His will to resolve the conflict between them was melting away with every minute that passed. His self-confidence dwindled. With a grunt, he opened the door and grabbed Lacey's suitcase from behind the seat.

He strode up the steps, practically running up the sidewalk.

The front door opened just as he lifted his hand to knock, and Kandy poked out her head. "Hey, thanks for bringing Lacey's stuff."

As Jared handed her the suitcase, unexpected relief washed over him. He was glad Lacey wasn't alone.

"How is she?"

"Sound asleep right now. She's been pretty out of

it since I picked her up at the clinic. You want to come in?" Kandy asked.

"I better get going," he said, turning away from her and heading back down the sidewalk.

Kandy shrugged and watched as he pulled away from the curb, then she carried the suitcase to Lacey's room.

"Hey, sleepyhead, are you awake? Your cowboy just dropped off your stuff."

Lacey pushed herself up on her elbows to look at Kandy. When she readjusted her injured foot on the stack of pillows at the end of her bed, a fresh jab of pain shot from her ankle to her shin. "Did he say anything?"

"He asked about you."

"Is that all?"

Kandy shot her a suspicious look. "What do you mean?"

"Nothing."

Kandy pursued. "Okay, what else happened at that cabin in the woods?"

Lacey groaned, her ankle throbbing.

"You hungry? Thirsty?" Kandy asked softly, her voice filled with concern.

"Some water. And another pain pill." Lacey's thoughts felt fuzzy, confused, her emotions raw.

"Here you go." Kandy sat on the edge of the bed, handing Lacey a glass and a brightly-colored capsule. "You feel like talking?"

Lacey swallowed the pill and lay back down, her eyes closed. She waited a few minutes for the pill to kick in. It made her feel relaxed; it made her feel like confiding. "We talked, had too much champagne and got . . . friendly, that's all."

"How friendly?" When Lacey didn't answer, Kandy

continued. "Something tells me that your year of celibacy ended last night. Am I right?"

Lacey forced her eyes open to look at Kandy. "I feel like an idiot," she whispered.

"Well, the way I see it, you can look at it two ways." Kandy's voice was low and soothing. "Chalk it up to mutual attraction. Two lonely adults, safe sex, a good time. Or," she continued quietly, "you need to figure out if there's more to it than that."

Lacey let her heavy eyelids close. *But was there more?* Maybe Kandy was right. She should just let it go.

"It's just," Lacey began, "that he's too complicated. I feel like I've finally gotten over Blake and Sean and then life pushes me together with another single father with a daughter that I could easily care about. I don't think I could handle another heartbreak."

"And . . ." Kandy urged.

"And it's not what I need or want right now." The words sounded weak, even to her.

"What makes you so sure it would end in heartbreak?"

"I don't want to take the chance," her voice trailed off. "I've thought through things a million times and I know what my life is and I certainly know what I *don't* want."

"You sure about that?" Kandy's voice sounded far away as the pain medication kicked in.

"He's not good for me," Lacey whispered.

Several moments passed in silence, and Lacey's mind began to feel deliciously numb.

"Feeling better? Is the pain lessening?" Kandy asked.

Lacey nodded. Kandy was sometimes more like a wise little sister than a prized employee, and she valued her friendship. She was glad she was there, glad to be able to confide in her.

Lacey's eyelids flew up. "Don't you have to get back to the salon?" She forced herself to pay attention.

"Nope, Sue came in to sub for me. Everything's fine. Hey, you got two calls yesterday."

"From?"

"The first one was from Corporate. The said they wanted to talk to you about that regional position in Denver. I'd be mad at you except they said if you took the job, they were considering *me* for the management position here—because you recommended me."

Lacey smiled as she allowed her eyes to close. "You're ready, even if you don't know it." *Denver.* New place, new job. The promotion she'd been waiting for. No Jared or Jamie to break her heart. A perfect solution to the mess she was in.

"And the second call?"

"The marketing manager wanted to know if you were going to make it to the annual meeting on Thursday evening."

Lacey groaned her response. "This Thursday?"

"I told her about your foot and she said she'd understand, but she hoped you'd go. The new general manager of the mall will be there and he wants to meet all the merchant managers."

It was an important meeting. Lacey had heard the new manager had remodeling plans that would affect about half of the store fronts, and she hoped hers was included. She caught her breath painfully as she readjusted her foot.

"You want me to tell her no?" Kandy asked.

"No, I'd better try to go. Go ahead and RSVP for me. I should be fine by then, at least enough to get through the business meeting. If my ankle bothers me, I'll just skip the dinner and dance part."

"Okay, boss."

Lacey sighed and contemplated what she could wear to the formal event that would draw the least attention to her bandaged foot. She knew she should attend the meeting. Even if she decided to take the Denver job offer, she still had her salon's best interest in mind.

She had also heard that the new manager was in the decision stages of which storefronts would *not* be included in the mall-funded facelift. This was the perfect chance to argue for the need to include the salon in the mall's plans.

Having made the decision, Lacey felt herself relax. Her body felt heavier as the pain medication's effect lulled her into a safe, dreamless sleep.

"Lacey? You asleep?" When she got no answer, Kandy tiptoed out of the bedroom, closing the door softly behind her.

Lacey pulled to a stop and allowed the valet attendant to help her out of her car. She forced a weak smile as she joined the crowd lined up at the entrance of the grand old Victorian hotel where the annual mall meeting was being held.

The men were in tuxedos or dark suits, and most of the women were in short black dresses, a few in formal silk pantsuits, with a fair number wearing sequined gowns. Her hand nervously smoothed the floorlength skirt of the powder blue gown she'd chosen, primarily because its length served to conceal her bandaged ankle. By keeping it covered, she hoped to avoid having to endlessly repeat the account of how her injury had occurred.

Every recounting induced a flood of unwanted emotion. There had been no word from Jared since the accident, and part of her was glad. It proved her suspicions that he wasn't serious, and confirmed her own decision that she just needed to chalk up the weekend to experience. Two consenting adults getting together, that was all.

Glancing downward, Lacey checked the position of her bodice. Her dress was strapless and formfitting, and she felt a little self-conscious about the amount of bare skin it exposed.

Her goal was to look sophisticated, confident, and professional. She'd had Kandy put her hair up in an elegant twisted braid, completing the look.

Lacey began to scan the crowd, noting familiar faces and running names through her mind. The marketing manager caught her gaze and waved, quickly approaching, her hands fluttering excitedly.

"Oh, Lacey, you made it. I'm so thrilled. How are you feeling? Great dress, by the way. Where did you find it? Now, come with me to meet Chad Watson, our new, quite handsome and eligible general manager. He's to die for." Her greeting gushed in one continuous vocalization.

Lacey didn't bother to reply to the woman, knowing any comment would fly in one ear and out the other, unnoticed. Clenching her teeth against a stab of pain, she controlled her limp as she followed behind the woman.

Deepening her smile in readiness, Lacey mentally rehearsed what she would say. She'd heard Watson was very bright, very young, and a keen executive who'd quickly climbed the corporate ladder. He also had a reputation for being a ruthless businessman.

She needed him on her side.

"Lacey Murdock manages the Shear Delight Salon. This is Chad Watson, our new general manager."

Lacey extended her hand, shocked to find an open, friendly face before her. Watson was not what she expected.

He was at least six feet tall, impeccably dressed in a white silk tuxedo with a collarless shirt, massive shoulders filling the coat. His skin was "just back from the tropics" tanned and his tawny gold hair pulled back in a ponytail. Brilliant blue eyes held her gaze as he grasped her hand.

"Great to meet you, Lacey, please call me Chad."

He was drop-dead gorgeous, which immediately put Lacey on edge. In the retail business, good looks frequently suggested an insufferable personality. She hoped he was different.

"I'm looking forward to showing you the salon and convincing you to include us in the remodeling." Might as well be upfront, she decided. For a long moment he studied her intently, his eyes sharp and assessing.

Finally, he released her hand. His gaze unwavering, he said, "Martha, please see that Lacey is at my table so we can talk a little business during dinner." His tone was a unique mixture of warmth and cool authority.

Powerful relief filled Lacey as she enjoyed the satisfaction of so quickly securing his attention. The evening might prove to be even more successful than she'd hoped.

The business meeting finally over, Chad joined Lacey's table, taking the empty chair beside her. From his speech, she'd learned that the future changes for the mall included a ten million dollar expansion.

To everyone's surprise, Chad's concise address had been humorous, to the point, and optimistic. Recurrent cheerful applause interrupted his words as he described the modifications and improvements already planned.

As he settled himself at the table, Chad greeted each guest by name, then ceremoniously placed the dinner napkin in his lap.

"I'm afraid your entree is probably cold," Lacey began, "but they insisted on leaving it and . . ."

Before she could finish her thought, Chad had raised a finger toward the catering captain. Within moments he was served a fresh entree.

A sense of the man's strength and authority came to her, even though he had been both gracious and pleasant about his request for a hot entree. It was obvious the man had expectations and standards for every part of his life.

Lacey stared at him, watching his interaction with the others. How old was he? She figured him to be close to her age, early thirties, though he could even be late twenties, she realized.

With a start, Lacey also realized that Chad Watson seemed to have every quality, physical and otherwise, of her imagined "perfect" man, and precisely fit her list of must-haves. He was young, successful, had a good job and, best of all, he seemed nicely uncomplicated. So different from Jared, she thought.

Lacey cocked her head to examine his features. Yes, he was dazzling, but why didn't her heart skip a beat when she looked at him? She shrugged off her lack of attraction and attributed it to the distraction of her throbbing ankle.

In his speech, Chad had described his own path of achievement and stability, sharing his personal and business philosophies. On the personal front, he had even declared his lifestyle did not include a wife . . . yet.

Chad interrupted her thoughts. "I've examined the profit and loss statements for the salon since you've been the manager, Lacey. Quite impressive." He turned toward her and leaned forward, lowering his voice. "I'm already considering the salon for remodeling, but I wanted to meet you and learn more about the accomplished businesswoman who turned things around during the last fiscal year."

Lacey looked at him with amused wonder, beaming at his kind words and approval. This was no cut-throat executive, this was an intelligent, serious, self-assured man. Definitely financially secure, she thought, mentally checking off another perfect trait. *And* a man who appreciates the efforts of a career woman, she added.

Nothing like Jared. She winced at the unwanted emotion that tugged at her heart. Silently she listened to the conversation at the table as it focused on local business trends, city politics, and the turmoil of the retail industry.

It was an environment where she was decidedly comfortable, Lacey thought, smiling at the ease Chad had in answering difficult questions. He was certainly focused on the bottom line, but appeared to at least be willing to consider some of the merchants' suggestions.

Not so stubborn. Much more open-minded than most men she knew. With some effort, she pushed away another thought of Jared. *Stop comparing them,* she commanded herself.

Laughter burst from the people at the table, bringing Lacey's attention back to the present. Chad joined the others, his laugh deep, warm, and rich.

He brought his napkin to his lips, then turned to Lacey, a small smile on his face.

"Do you think I've won them over yet?" he asked in a low, composed voice.

Lacey nodded. He had. And easily.

He gazed at her speculatively, adding, "I won't be staying for the dancing tonight—I'm not interested in music and I'm afraid dancing is a frivolity I loathe. I'd like to finish our conversation tomorrow. Are you free for lunch?"

She watched the subtle play of emotions on his face. Was he asking if she was free for lunch . . . or *free* for lunch? Her eyes clouded for just an instant. Why not?

SIXTEEN

Lacey sat waiting for Chad to return to their table in the Haut Monde, folding and refolding the napkin in her lap. She was surprised and annoyed at her nervousness. It was just a business lunch, she rationalized, trying to convince herself she was being foolish, overreacting to his attention.

She glanced around the dining room, noticing mostly couples with their heads together, sipping on afternoon espressos or glasses of wine.

"Hope you haven't been waiting long," Chad said, sitting down next to her.

She smiled and shook her head.

"I ordered for us on the way in," he said. "Hope you don't mind."

Lacey checked the feeling of vexation she experienced. Why should it annoy her that he had ordered without asking, she wondered. It was something that suited Chad, she decided, shrugging off the mood.

As he sat down, Chad's gaze rested on the group at the next table, a couple with a well-behaved toddler and an infant asleep in a carrier in the chair closest to his. Chad's brows drew together in an angry frown. "I specifically asked to *not* be placed near children," he said. "Such an annoyance, especially during a business lunch."

Lacey noted his set face, his clamped mouth and fixed eyes. He was genuinely bothered by the close proximity of the charming little family.

"So," he said, redirecting his gaze to her, "where shall we begin?"

"Have you made final decisions about which stores will be getting a facelift?" she asked, her voice fading, distracted by the plate of raw oysters the waiter placed in front of each of them.

She watched as Chad eagerly squeezed lemon over his plate, then looked at her, waiting. The look and smell of the raw shellfish nauseated her.

"I checked and they were just flown in today, quite fresh."

Lacey picked up a lemon wedge with shaking fingers, hoping he didn't notice. *This is ridiculous. Just tell him you think they're disgusting.* Why did she suddenly feel inferior? A little too unworldly?

The waiter arrived with a bottle of wine, pulling Chad's gaze from her for a moment, providing the opportunity for Lacey to carefully slip one of the oysters out of its shell and into the napkin on her lap.

Chad ceremoniously sniffed the cork and sipped a little of the wine. A small scowl replaced his dazzling smile. "Sorry, Fletcher, that won't quite do. Please bring me an '84."

The waiter gave him a nod and pivoted away.

Chad smiled comfortably to himself. "They'll learn that my tastes are quite specific. So, back to business, then. To answer what you really want to know, yes, the salon is included in the plan."

"I'm so glad." Lacey was genuinely pleased, knowing her hard work had paid off in more ways than the offer of a regional promotion. Corporate would be delighted at the confirmation of the news.

The waiter returned with another bottle of wine and Chad repeated his ritual, allowing Lacey to quickly slip the remaining two oysters off her plate and into her napkin.

As the waiter poured the merlot into two crystal glasses, his gaze caught hers for an instant.

"Excuse me, Mademoiselle, I noticed that your napkin is a bit frayed. Would you allow me to replace it for you?" His tone was apologetic.

"Of course," she said. *Saved.* She handed her napkin to him with a small, shy smile. As he placed a fresh cloth in her lap, amusement flickered in his eyes as they briefly met hers.

"Very good," he said, spinning quickly away from the table.

Lacey made a mental note of his name; her intention was to send a thank you with a free cut and style coupon enclosed. *What a classy guy.*

With barely controlled enthusiasm, Chad explained to Lacey that the owners and he had met several months ago regarding which storefronts would benefit from the remodeling. Now it was just a matter of informing those that had been selected and prepare for the disappointment of the merchants that had been excluded.

Lacey squelched the feeling of empathetic dissatisfaction she knew the merchants *not* included would surely feel. But this is just business, she reasoned.

"You seem a little distant." Chad caught her gaze and held it. "I hope you know our decisions are nothing personal. Everything is based on facts and figures, profit and loss."

Lacey nodded. She did know that some of the stores in the mall faced nonrenewal of their leases this year due to less than satisfactory sales quotas, but it was still difficult to think in terms of affecting people's livelihoods—and sometimes their lives—without even talking with them, taking into account that they were people, not just facts and figures.

The waiter returned with their entrees—fortunately nothing exotic—and Chad's conversation turned to small talk. He was very good at it, Lacey noticed, and she found herself tempted to reveal a bit more than she normally would to someone in his position of authority.

She frowned. There was something about him that made her slightly uncomfortable, guarded. Perhaps it was just his demeanor, she considered. He was so organized, focused, determined not to allow anything—or anyone, for that matter—to interfere with his plans.

Perhaps it was his lack of spontaneity, or his obvious dislike for children, and dancing. Lacey smirked behind her napkin, imagining him in a cowboy hat and boots. Impossible, but amusing, she thought.

Lacey glanced at her watch. "I've really got to get back to the salon. Thanks so much for all the positive feedback," she said.

Chad's face broke into a leisurely smile. "Glad we

could spend some time together. I expect it to become a regular habit, Lacey."

She returned his smile, turning away from him before he noticed her blazing cheeks. He was just a bit too sure of himself, she thought.

Hurrying as much as her ankle would allow, Lacey made her way back to the salon, knowing her client would be waiting for her at the shampoo bowl.

Jared paced restlessly in front of Shear Delight, a bouquet of wildflowers in one hand, an envelope in the other. The entire way there he'd rehearsed what to say, but now his mind was a blank.

When Joann had heard about how he left Lacey alone on the trail and then how she'd injured her ankle, she'd read him the riot act. His sister was a master at pouring salt in his wounds, but in the end, he'd admitted how he felt about Lacey.

She'd altered her role, then, to sympathetic big sister, carefully reminding him to look at the big picture, consider his options, encouraging him to consider some sort of compromise.

Jared stretched his neck and rotated his shoulders. He was exhausted. Five consecutive sleepless nights were taking their toll. Every night he'd tossed and turned, wondering what to do, and now he found himself wandering aimlessly in front of Lacey's salon, clueless.

A bead of sweat stung his eye. *Geez, why did she affect him so much?* Jared stopped his pacing and wiped his forehead with the back of his hand. Might as well get it over with.

* * *

Lacey plopped down in the chair at the appointment desk, grateful to check out her last client. Her ankle throbbed beneath the elastic bandage, and she elevated it on a box that she'd hidden under the desk. She considered the possibility that she might have come back to work a little too early.

The doctor had recommended a week off, but after the mall dinner, she'd had an overwhelming burst of positive energy. Besides, she missed the nurturing environment of the busy salon.

Plus, she reminded herself, she'd had a lunch date. Business meeting, she corrected.

Chad *was* easy to talk to, and she'd been pleased with his relaxed manner and evident business savvy. He was indeed as shrewd and bright as he appeared.

She'd also learned he spent a great deal of time in Denver, perhaps an added plus. He'd seemed genuinely disappointed to learn of her decision to leave the area, but impressed at her drive to climb the corporate ladder.

All in all, she felt it had been an interesting experience. When he asked if she would like to keep in touch once she'd moved, she'd said yes quite easily. She pulled a small card from her pocket, Chad's personal card, imprinted with his name and a Denver phone number.

He'd made her promise to call him the minute she was settled. She decided she probably would.

Denver. A new life, one filled with responsibility and devoid of the complicated feelings she had for Jared. In many ways, staying home with her sore ankle had been a blessing in disguise. It had provided the opportunity to think, reevaluate her goals and reaffirm the criteria she assured herself were legitimate.

She felt good about her call to the corporate office

that morning, when she'd formally accepted the promotion that would take her away from San Diego, away from Jared and Jamie.

An unexpected shudder accompanied the thought, and there was a heavy feeling in her stomach. Denver would be an adventure, she told herself, forcing the nagging picture of Jared from her consciousness.

At the sound of a check being torn from its holder, Lacey returned her attention to her client. "Thanks, Marge, call Kandy for an appointment in about a month to trim the ends off—your perm will last longer."

She handed a receipt and a reminder card to her customer. "I'd get up, but my ankle is really throbbing."

The woman clucked sympathetically and patted her new hairstyle. "You get some rest, Lacey. I'm really going to miss you. I hope Kandy does as good a job."

"She will. I promise—or I'll come back and torment her."

The woman turned away, chuckling.

Standing behind her, stone-faced, was Jared.

Lacey lifted her chin and met his neutral gaze.

"How's your ankle?" he said.

"Much better. Thanks for bringing my suitcase over the other day. Sorry I was too out of it to thank you then."

Jared stared at her. *Had he heard right? Why did that blue-haired lady say she was going to miss Lacey?*

"Those for me?" Lacey asked, standing up behind the counter, her hand extended. "They're beautiful. Are they from the yard?"

Dumbfounded, he nodded. "And this is from

Jamie. It's an invitation to her birthday party on Saturday. I promised to deliver it to you."

Lacey brought the flowers to her nose, breathing deeply. "Reminds me of the mountain air," she said, her voice sounding overly cheerful. "Is the party this Saturday, or next?"

"Next," he answered. "You're probably working and—"

"I'd love to come." Lacey turned and got Kandy's attention. "Kandy, would you get some water for these, and the other vase that's in the back?"

Kandy waved from the back of the salon, then ducked into the back room. She returned with a crystal vase, half filled with water.

Lacey put the flowers in the vase and placed them next to a vase that already took up half the countertop, a vase that held a dozen red roses.

Jared stared at the two bouquets. It was almost ludicrous, the contrast between the scraggly wildflowers and the perfect long-stemmed beauties. While Lacey rearranged his flowers, he glanced at the gift card that was displayed among the roses: *I really enjoyed our lunch—looking forward to Denver. Chad.*

"Hey, Jared, have you heard the good news? Lacey's been promoted. She's the new regional supervisor of our Denver salons." Kandy's voice stabbed through the thick silence.

Jared stared first at Kandy and then at Lacey. "So, you're leaving then?"

"In a few weeks. I have to get some things situated. Give notice to my landlord. Train Kandy to replace me . . ." Her voice trailed off.

"I see." Jared forced his voice to stay neutral, though his heart thudded loudly in his ears. His body betrayed him, reacting with a vengeance. Sweat trickled down his face and his stomach tightened into a painful knot.

Lacey looked away. "It's a great job. A big change for me." She paused, as though she were searching for the right words. "It's what I've been working so diligently for."

"Right. Well, if you're too busy for the party I'm sure Jamie will understand."

"I'll be there," she said softly.

Jared forced a smile, then turned away.

"Thanks for the flowers," she called after him. He didn't turn to answer her and Lacey watched him until he got lost in the crowd of shoppers.

"Nice bouquet," Kandy said.

"Nice," Lacey repeated. She felt a sudden, very intense sense of loss.

"You okay?" Kandy asked.

"Just tired. My foot really hurts. Do you mind closing up tonight? I'm beat."

"Happy to, boss, it'll be good practice."

Lacey smiled at Kandy's enthusiasm. She remembered that feeling—excited and ready for new challenges, ready for something new. She felt a different version of it now. She'd worked hard, her successes coming because of it. Now she felt ready for a new life, new challenges, an adventure.

Denver would be the opportunity she'd been waiting for. More money, more responsibility, the chance to climb the corporate ladder. And Chad, she reminded herself, pensively wondering how things would play out.

"If you're ready to go, let me walk you out to your car," Kandy suggested.

Lacey pulled her purse from under the desk and nodded. "Let's go."

They walked silently through the mall and Lacey's pace was slow. She didn't try to control her limp, instead focused on keeping a smile on her face during the painful trek to the parking lot.

Kandy broke the ice. "So, are you going to explain the roses or am I going to have to drag it out of you?"

Lacey smiled. "It was just a business lunch."

"And what about the *looking forward to Denver* part?"

"Chad spends a lot of time in Denver, so we might see each other there, that's all."

"He's quite a looker," Kandy urged.

"He's nice, though, and I think he'll be good for the mall. He's got a good, level head on his shoulders. He's ambitious and he's one of those men who can see the big picture, you know?"

"Sounds a little boring to me," Kandy said, "all work and no play. Busy making money and being successful. No time for life."

Lacey listened to the comments, realizing they rang true. Chad was intelligent, interesting, handsome, young, uncomplicated. She rattled off the traits that should be making her swoon instead of feeling hesitant.

"Well, the roses tell me he's very interested in you," Kandy said as they left the mall and headed toward the employee parking lot.

"I guess so," Lacey replied in a low, composed voice.

"Don't sound so enthusiastic," Kandy said. "What's really bothering you, Lacey?"

Lacey paused. What *was* bothering her? "No sparks. No chemistry. At least not yet."

"And Jared?" Kandy urged.

"Too complicated."

"But sparks, am I right?"

Lacey sighed. Definitely sparks, she thought.

"Well, all I know is that the chemistry is a vital part of the relationship, Lacey, and my advice—whether you want it or not—is to hold out for the sparks." Kandy blurted out the words fast and furious. "Those fireworks can help you get through the difficult times a lot better than complete compatibility."

Lacey stared at her, astonished at how valid her words sounded. But Kandy was young, she rationalized, and in love. The infatuation stage was fun and intoxicating, she knew that. And even though Kandy's words held a grain of truth, she was convinced the mature way to consider life's choices had more to do with shared goals than passion in the bedroom.

As they reached Lacey's car, Kandy shook her head in frustration. "I know I've got a big mouth sometimes, but you know I just care about you, right?"

Lacey flashed a broad smile. "Of course, Kandy. Don't worry, I'm a big girl and I'm fine, really."

After a quick hug, Lacey dropped into the driver's seat and headed for her little house.

With one hand, she rubbed at the tension headache centered between her eyes, eager to take some pain medication and get to bed early.

There was much to be done in the next few weeks and Lacey found she was actually looking forward to the business of packing and planning her trip. It was certainly what she needed to keep her mind occupied and as far away from Jared as possible.

It was the perfect solution, she reminded herself, the thought becoming a mantra during her drive home.

As she pulled her car to the curb in front of her

house, Lacey wondered how she had gotten there. Her mind felt numb and she realized she must have kicked into autopilot. Thankfully, she'd made it home safely.

She sat in the car for a moment, gathering the strength she would need to get out and handle the rest of the walk to her front door. Her heart jumped to her throat as she reacted to the unexpected sound of sharp rapping on the car window.

A woman with unnaturally white-blonde hair was bent over to look at her through the window, trying to get her attention.

Puzzled, Lacey opened her door and stepped out to look at the woman over the roof of the car. "Can I help you?" she asked gingerly, thinking perhaps the woman needed directions or the use of her phone.

"Actually, I just wanted to meet you. You're Lacey, right? Jamaica has told me so much about you that when I saw you leaving the salon, I'm afraid I decided to follow you home."

Lacey's brow furrowed. Then as casually as she could manage, she asked, "Are you Jamie's mother?"

The woman nodded, then awkwardly cleared her throat. "Marsha," she said in a honied voice. "I hope I didn't scare you. Like I said, I just wanted to meet you."

Lacey's thoughts bounced in her head, synchronizing with the painful throbbing of her ankle.

Even though her apprehension increased by the second, she quickly considered her options, deciding to talk to the woman. As she regarded the petite blonde, Lacey decided *she* was the one who looked frightened—and a little embarrassed.

"Would you like to come in for a minute? I'm afraid I have to get off my ankle for a while and take some medication." Lacey struggled to keep her voice friendly and noncommittal. She examined the woman's face for more clues.

"I promise not to keep you," the woman answered, a tentative smile forming on her lips.

"Follow me, then. That's my place up there." Lacey pointed at her house, shut the car door and led the way up the sidewalk.

Inside, as she snapped on the lights and entered the kitchen, the woman silently followed her and sat at the kitchen table.

Lacey busied herself getting a glass of water and forcing the top off her bottle of medication. Her fingers shook as she battled with the child-proof lid. Finally, she popped a capsule in her mouth and downed the entire glass of water, then turned to face Jared's ex-wife.

"Thanks for seeing me," Marsha began, her voice wavering a little in its tone. "Jamaica's hair was so different when I saw her recently and she just gushed about how wonderful you were. Then I found out about the weekend you spent with Jared . . ." Her voice trailed off.

Lacey sat at the table, waiting for the woman to get to some sort of point, to understand what kind of reason she had for taking the trouble to follow her home just to talk with her.

"We've been divorced for a while now," Marsha continued, "but of course I still have Jamaica's best interest in mind."

As she stared at her, Lacey found it difficult to take the woman's professed maternal instincts seriously. Her appearance, for one thing, more resembled the popular waiflike models of the fashion world. Her overly bleached hair was cut in a short, spiked style, and her makeup featured heavily lined eyes and pale lipstick. She wore a cropped top that revealed a pierced naval and the edge of a brightly colored tattoo.

Lacey had even more trouble picturing Jared and the woman together. She was an unbelievable contrast to him, a thoroughly modern young woman linked with an impossibly old-fashioned, conservative man. It simply didn't jibe.

"So, what can I do for you?" Lacey asked, wishing the conversation was over, regretting now she'd been polite and invited the woman in.

"I'm really not sure," Marsha began. "I guess I just wanted to see what kind of woman you were. Don't get me wrong, I'm not a bit interested in Jared anymore. He's a good father to Jamaica and she's much happier up on that wretched mountain and around those stinking animals."

Lacey's eyes narrowed as she stared at Marsha.

"I guess I just wanted to warn you about how awful it is up there, so isolated from anything modern and convenient. I didn't want you to be . . . fooled, like I was."

"I see," Lacey replied. She could feel the pain medication taking hold, her eyes glazing a little as she focused on Marsha's pale pink lips.

"And I wanted to warn you about Jared's stubborn streak and how stifling he can be. You look like a successful woman, and I just wanted you to know what to expect—how bullheaded Jared can be about women working, I mean."

Lacey rubbed her temples. "Thanks, but Jared and I aren't seeing each other. We just won the weekend through the auction and decided to go through with it for the sake of the publicity for the charity involved."

Marsha's eyes studied her intensely. "Oh. I guess I just sort of jumped to conclusions."

"No harm done." Lacey stood up, hoping Marsha would take the hint to leave.

Marsha stood and smiled weakly. "Well, thanks for being so nice to me. Maybe you can do my hair some time."

Lacey turned away without replying. *Was the woman nuts?* She bit down hard on her lower lip to prevent herself from lecturing the woman on how she had thrown away a perfectly good life and a darling little girl for the so-called glamour of her career. Didn't she realize that, these days, women handled both?

At the door, she watched as Marsha drove off in a bright red sports car. "Yes," she whispered, "Jared is a good father to your little one, and I hope you don't discover, when you're old and gray, how much you missed by not being there for her yourself."

Even in her dazed anger, Lacey felt a little sorry for Marsha.

SEVENTEEN

"Daaaa-dy, Auntie Jo is here."

Jamie's lilting voice interrupted Jared's concentration. "Ask her to fix you something to eat." He needed just a few more minutes to finish trimming Dolly's toenails. He had saved her for last so he could take his time.

"There, there," he cooed, "just one more nip." Dolly was his oldest and favorite llama and had produced quite a brood of offspring, progeny easy to sell due to their good temperament and lustrous coats.

Returning her foot to the ground, Jared stroked the llama's neck, murmuring softly. She brought her nose to his neck, sniffing delicately. "Yes, you are my favorite," he reassured her in a soothing voice. "Now, go tend to your little one."

Jared watched as the gentle creature crossed the pen to return to her offspring, who was anxiously waiting to nurse. Checking his watch, he realized he had just enough time to shower and get to the Rockin' Ranch before the first set. Glenn was back playing bass with the group but had asked him to fill in every other Friday so he could spend more time with his new baby girl.

Jared understood how precious that time was. He'd loved every stage of his daughter's life, including her infancy. Now she was getting ready to start school. Amazing, he thought. He had the unmistakable feeling that time was slipping away much too quickly.

At the back porch he unlaced his work boots and left them outside. Joann was in the kitchen stir frying vegetables and shrimp.

"Smells good," he said.

"Are you eating with us?" she asked. "Everything will be ready in about ten minutes."

"I'll shower quick," he said with a grin, walking down the hall toward the bathroom.

As he passed the doorway to Jamie's room, she called out, "Do you think she's coming?"

"Who?"

"Daa-ad. You know. The lady who cut my hair, the

Lacey lady." She sent him a "get serious" look that imitated her Aunt Jo perfectly.

"So sorry." He bent to ruffle her hair. "She said she would. We'll have to wait and see."

"But the party's tomorrow. Can't you call her and ask her?" Her eyes widened, her voice sweet.

Jared winced. By the tone in her voice it was apparent that Lacey's presence at Jamie's fifth birthday party was vital. "We'll see, sweetie, now Daddy's got to take a shower and go to work. I think Auntie Jo could use some help setting the table, okay?"

"Okay. I hope she comes, that's all."

"So do I, Jamie." He was surprised that his answer was really true. He *did* hope she came to the party. He wanted to say a proper goodbye. Because it would be goodbye, he reminded himself. The fact was that he would most likely never see Lacey Murdock again.

In the days since he'd seen Lacey at the salon, Jared had rationalized how her move to Denver would simplify everything. No decisions remained for him to make. She had already done that.

There was also a comprehension of relief. Her decision certainly released him from the onus of confessing his feelings about her, and at least he now knew precisely how diametrically opposed their feelings were.

The days had dragged since he'd seen her, and though Jared had found he'd been able to control his thoughts during the day, the nights had been difficult. Over and over he'd dreamed heart-pounding versions of their passionate night together. In his dreams, they'd made love everywhere in the secluded mountain cabin—in the hot tub, in the four-poster, in the kitchen, even outside under the tall pines.

Each morning he'd awakened, still reeling from

her fragrance, the memory of her touch, the thought of her. Each morning he shrugged off the delicious remnants of the unwanted dreams. Dreams of her.

As he stepped into the shower, he allowed his thoughts to create a picture of her in his mind. Immediately, his groin ached in response. Shaking his head, he knew it would just take time, time to get over the nagging, painful question about what might have been.

"Thanks for being such a good sport," Kandy said, her voice increasing in volume to compete with the music that commenced as she and Lacey walked in the door of the Rockin' Ranch. "Everyone really wanted to get together one last time before you got too busy getting ready to move."

Lacey nodded. She noticed Hank had been replaced at the door with a rather homely, serious-looking older man. *Probably much safer,* she thought, her stomach clenching at the memory of good old Hank. She shuddered.

She'd learned a lot from the experience, lessons she hoped to never repeat. She was in control of her life now. Her plans were materializing, just as she'd visualized—new job, new environment. It was just what she needed. The nagging pang of loneliness would disappear, she knew, as soon as she was on her way. As soon as she was far enough away.

"Hey, Lacey!" Gloria's voice came out of the crowd ahead of them and she managed to work her way through the mob to meet them.

"Hi, Gloria. How was your sister's wedding?" Lacey asked.

"Thanks to you, I looked *better* than the bride. I

hear you got some big promotion and you're movin', huh?"

Lacey nodded. "Time to try something new."

"Well, my hair and I will miss you terribly. Kandy, some of the gals are already at the reserved table on the dance floor." Gloria pointed, then twirled to service a table of customers.

"C'mon, Lacey, follow me and be careful of your foot," said Kandy as she blazed a trail toward the dance floor.

Lacey avoided looking at the stage, suppressing the part of her that hoped Jared was playing, even though she knew Friday nights were not his usual night to substitute for Glenn.

Even though she hadn't seen him since the day he'd shown up at the salon, her nights had been restless because of him, filled with strange dreams—endless walks toward mountains that kept moving further away; running through airports unable to find the right departure gate; even Jamie's sweet little face, tears on her pink cheeks.

Shaking off the unwanted feeling of sadness, Lacey forced a smile, returning her attention to the going-away party. She waved at the table filled with stylists from the salon, with the addition of several other women she knew from the mall.

The chair they'd saved for her placed her back to the band. Before she sat down, though, she snuck a peek at the stage, quickly locating the bass player. *Looks like Glenn's back.* She shrugged off the disappointment and concentrated on trying to hear the conversation at the table.

But she couldn't really pay attention. She excused herself quickly, headed for the bathroom, then took a quick left out the back door. *Where all my troubles began,* she thought. She closed her eyes, breathing in the warm, humid night air. A silvery slice of moon hung in the sky.

The volume of the band at a more acceptable level, she hummed along with the familiar tune, then noticed the faint sounds of a guitar playing along with the band. As she followed the sound, she finally made out the familiar profile of Jared's pickup. He was sitting on the end of the tailgate, long legs swinging as he picked the strings.

Lacey stared at him, instantly feeling both nostalgic and flustered. Slowly she walked down the steps of the deck. There was no reason not to, she argued. She should be sociable. She was an adult. It would be rude not to say hello, she told herself.

Jared turned his head at the sound of her footsteps, his fingers freezing on the strings of the guitar.

"Mind if I join you?" she asked.

"I see your ankle is better. I'm glad." His voice was low and soft.

"Are you playing tonight?"

"Well, I thought I was. Glenn said there was some sort of mix-up, but told me to stick around anyway. I was just hanging out for a while, to give Jo a chance to finish Jamie's bedtime ritual before I head back home. She loves to tuck her in." He paused before continuing. "You here with somebody?"

"A whole tableful of wild women." Lacey smiled. It felt good to talk to him. Natural. Normal.

Jared returned her smile.

"Kandy's idea of a farewell party," she explained.

"I see."

Lacey's gaze rested on the guitar. "I'd like to hear you play. I didn't get a chance to, when we were . . ."

Her voice faded. *When we were together.* Her cheeks flushed with sudden heat as she sat down next to him.

This time when she breathed, it was Jared's scent that filled her lungs—such a nice, clean smell, with the familiar hint of apricots. A gentle quiver began between her thighs as he began to strum. It felt like he was strumming her.

"Any requests?" he asked softly.

"Whatever you like." She looked into his eyes until he turned away, returning his attention to his fingers forming chords on the fretboard.

"This is one of Jamie's favorites," he said.

Lacey listened, her eyes closed. He was good, and she wondered if he'd been playing long. It made her realize that there was so much she didn't know about Jared Conrad, so much that she would never know.

Jared ended the tune with a series of chiming harmonics, the forefinger of his left hand straight, bouncing nimbly up and down the fretboard.

"That was beautiful. What was it?"

"My version of 'Blue Skies,' " he answered.

"I love acoustic guitar," she murmured.

Jared stood the guitar on his knee. He hadn't expected to see her at the club. At least at this moment, he realized, he was glad to be with her, even if his stomach was knotted painfully. And he was pleased she enjoyed his music, though he knew it shouldn't make any difference. Lacey was short term. So *what* if she liked his music?

"Here you are," Kandy declared. She stood on the deck, her hands on her hips. "Hey, Lacey, Luke's about to play a request in your honor and I'm afraid he would be pretty insulted if you didn't dance—maybe Jared could help you out. You do dance, don't you, Jared?"

Dance? With Lacey? Now?

Lacey looked at him, a weak smile on her lips. She shrugged, waiting for his answer.

"Sure, no problem." He packed his guitar and stowed it in the truck behind the seat. Kandy and Lacey stood on the deck, waiting for him.

As they walked through the back door, Luke's voice bellowed over the PA system. "And the next tune tonight is dedicated to Lacey Murdock, best little hairdresser in San Diego. They tell me she's thinkin' about leaving us and takin' her magic scissors to the Rocky Mountains. This one's for you, Lacey."

Luke gave a one-and-two-and to the band and they began playing a slow, romantic version of Buddy Holly's "True Love Waits."

Jared caught Lacey's gaze. *Did she recognize it?* His own musical memory immediately told him it was the song they had danced to—the night he'd removed his wedding ring, the night he'd driven her home and they'd argued.

If she did remember, there was no visible sign. Lacey reached for his hand as they made their way to the dance floor, already packed with dancers.

Jared's heart began a steady thump. Maybe this wasn't such a good idea, he thought. Finding a tiny space, he pulled her toward him, right hand at her waist, the other gingerly holding her right hand as though it might break if he squeezed it.

They began to sway with the music, unable to make much progress around the crowded dance floor. "Your ankle okay?" he whispered.

Lacey nodded. "Fine."

Glancing to his left, Jared saw a couple two-stepping dangerously close to them, forcing him to pull Lacey closer. She looked up at him, her eyes questioning him. "Sorry, that couple was about to collide with us."

After the couple passed, she didn't pull away from him. Holding her closely, he felt her uneven breathing.

Jared moved his hand from Lacey's waist to her back. Slipping under her silky hair, his hand rested on bare skin. *Her dress was backless. Geez.* He wondered if she had any idea what the touch of her skin did to him.

She snuggled closer to him, sending his pulse pounding. He hardened instantly and prayed she wouldn't notice. *Just a dance,* he reminded himself.

Her nearness was kindling a dangerous fire, and he knew it.

At the final verse, he loosened his hold on her, his heart aching. *Don't want what you can't have,* he told himself.

The song ended and they separated to join in the applause. Before Lacey could turn to look at him, he had already turned away, heading for the back door.

EIGHTEEN

Leaning her elbow on the kitchen table, Lacey rested her chin in her hand, her other hand mindlessly stirring a steaming mug of coffee. It was her third cup. The Friday night with the girls at the Rockin' Ranch had been a long one. One with too many rounds, too many toasts to good times, too many rehashed memories. Thankfully, she'd had the foresight to move her Saturday clients to Sunday. She had the entire day to herself.

As she brought the liquid to her lips, she closed her eyes. Aspirin and caffeine had finally taken the edge off her headache. The ache in her heart was another story.

It had been another restless night. This time, Jared had saturated her dreams. His hands, his lips, his body.

A heaviness centered in Lacey's chest as she sat in lonely silence. Her dazed stare moved from the window to an envelope on the table. *Jamie's birthday party invitation.*

She knew she should go. Jamie was depending on it—at least that's what Jared had implied. She picked up the envelope and pulled out the invitation. It was a glittery picture of a castle, complete with a princess waving from its tower.

> *The princess respectfully asks for your presence on the very important occasion of her fifth birthday.*

Lacey sighed. She knew it wouldn't take much to fall in love with Jamie. They'd hit it off like crazy the night of Joann's impromptu barbecue, sharing girl talk and secrets when she'd tucked her into bed.

Lacey listened to the clock chime eleven. She'd have just enough time to clean up and be there by one. It wouldn't be fair to Jamie if she didn't go, she decided.

Lacey ignored the little voice in her head that laughed at her logic. She even had a gift ready, an old typesetter's tray, ideal for hanging on the wall to display the little girl's collection of rocks and other natural treasures.

It's just a little girl's party. She probably wouldn't

even have to talk to Jared. He'd be busy with the other kids and things, she reasoned.

She finished her coffee and put her breakfast dishes in the sink. At least with a destination in mind, her morning began to feel like it had a purpose.

"She's here! Lacey's here!" Jamie's voice called out from the driveway.

Jared finished checking Dolly's saddle, then looked up to confirm his daughter's announcement. A little boy was sitting quietly on the llama's back, waiting patiently for him to lead Dolly around the pen. Jared had been giving rides for over an hour and this was the last one.

"Good girl, Dolly," he murmured. The llama had endured each child with tenderness and grace, and he was grateful for her gentle disposition. She was used to Jamie, but he hadn't been sure she would react as kindly toward a dozen pint-sized, wiggly visitors.

The party was going well. Joann had already gotten everyone fed, and was in the gazebo making ice cream in an old-fashioned ice cream maker. Some of the kids were turning the crank while others set out dishes and all the fixings for make-your-own sundaes.

Each had ridden Dolly and, with great pride, Jamie had seen to it that everyone had toured the barn to see her kittens and then to jump in the hay.

Jared's stomach clenched as he deliberately kept his attention away from the driveway, avoiding Lacey's arrival.

He patted Dolly's neck. "Last one, girl, almost done."

The little boy sat stiffly in the saddle as Jared led the llama in a large circle. The boy had been reluctant to ride the creature, but had relented at the last minute when Jared assured him how much Dolly enjoyed giving rides.

Jared glanced at the little boy. He was smiling now, much more relaxed, even taking one hand off the saddlehorn to wave at the other children.

As they arrived at the starting point, the little boy grinned. "That was fun! Can we go again?"

Jared looked up to see Lacey following Jamie into the house. "Sure," he answered, grateful to lead Dolly forward for another loop around her pen.

"Do you want to open your present now?" Lacey asked, sitting on the edge of the bed. Jamie had insisted she come to her room to show off how clean it was.

Jamie nodded, sending her auburn curls bouncing. "And I have one for you, too," she said.

"But it's *your* birthday," Lacey said, drawing her eyebrows together in a lighthearted frown. "How come *I* get a present?"

Jamie shrugged, her eyes flashing.

"Well, you go first," Lacey said, handing Jamie the large, tissue-wrapped bundle.

Jamie carefully opened the package, setting the tissue paper aside. Her eyes grew wide as she examined the wooden box with its different-sized compartments.

Lacey waited. She was enjoying watching Jamie's mind work. She could see the little girl determining what the box might be for. Before long, the light shone in her eyes when an idea finally formed.

"It's for my c'llection, isn't it? I can put my rocks in this part, my feathers here, and my sticks in here . . ."

"You like it?" Lacey asked, pleased that Jamie had

figured it out for herself. She was a bright girl. "You can hang it on the wall or lay it flat on a table." She showed Jamie the picture hanger she'd put on the back of the tray.

"It's perfect. Thank you very, very much." Jamie threw her arms around Lacey's neck for a hug.

She drew the little girl closer and rocked her in a loving, maternal embrace. She bit her lip until it throbbed like her pulse, shocked at the wave of emotions that threatened to overpower her. "I'm glad you like it. I hoped you would."

"Wait till Daddy sees it," she said. "I bet he likes it almost as much as me."

Lacey nodded and studied Jamie's face: her mouth in an irresistible smile, gray-green eyes sparkling, shiny strawberry blonde curls against cheeks with a peaches-and-cream complexion. *An angel.* She felt a tug on her heart.

"I almost forgot," Jamie said as she turned away. She went to her closet and retrieved a small box, childishly wrapped in wrinkled, obviously recycled paper, that was sprinkled with pink ponies and fairies.

Lacey held the charming little package in one hand. "I wonder what it is," she said. Winking at Jamie, first she smelled it, then shook it, then held it to her ear.

"Open it, open it," Jamie urged. "I made it for you."

"Ah, a clue. Hmm. It's not very heavy and it doesn't make any noise, so I guess it's not a box of jewels, is it?"

Jamie shook her head, giggling behind her fist.

"I guess I better open it, then." Lacey pulled at the paper.

"Daddy, come watch Lacey open the present I made her."

Lacey's fingers stopped. She looked up to see Jared lounging casually against the door frame.

"What present?" he asked.

By his expression of wariness, Lacey suspected he was unaware of Jamie's gift for her. She held up the box for him to see.

Jared shrugged matter-of-factly and shook his head, confirming her theory.

Lacey stared at him. He was wearing the same forest green shirt and faded jeans he'd worn during the photo shoot at the cabin. He looked devastatingly handsome as he stood in the doorway, his gaze locked on hers.

She licked her lips when he ran his fingers through his hair, pushing back an errant curl from his forehead.

A delicious shiver ran through her. His mere presence in the room had an instant impact on her. *Did he feel it too?*

Jamie sighed loudly, obviously frustrated at the slow progress in the opening of the gift.

Lacey swallowed hard and tore her gaze from Jared's. With trembling fingers she finished removing the paper and opened the white box. In a bed of cotton balls was a gold-painted, long half of a broken wishbone.

Lacey took the wishbone from the box and realized it actually was meant to be a pendant.

"The necklace part is yarn that I crocheted," Jamie explained, "and it's made from our llamas' wool. I even put some beads on it and everything," she said proudly. "Auntie Jo helped a little."

Lacey held the necklace up, running her fingers over the crocheted yarn. It was remarkably soft and delicate, similar to mohair. Multicolored ceramic beads were strung on either side of the wishbone. She looked up as Jared walked in the room and stood at the end of the bed.

"Oh, Jamie. It's beautiful. Shall I put it on?" Lacey gazed at Jamie. The little girl looked as though she might burst with joy. How simple life was at five.

Lacey put the necklace over her head. "It fits perfectly."

Jamie reached up to delicately touch the wishbone. "I saved it all the way from last Thanksgiving. You 'member, Daddy?"

Lacey looked at Jared's face. The hard lines softened when he looked at his daughter. He nodded.

"I remember, sweetpea. You got the long half, but you said you were saving your wish."

"Right. And now I made a wish." Jamie fingered the wishbone gently. "You wanna know my wish?" she whispered dramatically, looking first at her father, then at Lacey.

Lacey nodded, mesmerized by the compelling look in Jamie's eyes

"I wished for you to be my new mom." Her hushed voice had a ring of finality, as though she believed with all her heart that her wish would be granted.

Lacey gasped, her heart thudding in her ears. She was speechless in her surprise. She dropped her gaze to the wishbone that hung ceremoniously around her neck.

Jared cleared his throat. "Jamie, Auntie Jo told me she could use your help with the ice cream. Why don't you go and see what she needs, okay?"

"Okay, Daddy." She looked at Lacey and asked, "You're staying for ice cream, aren't you?"

"Of course, it's your birthday." Lacey managed to

keep her voice light and cheerful, amazed that she could make her lips work at all.

"See ya," Jamie called as she skipped out of the room.

Lacey felt the bed shift under Jared's weight as he sat beside her on Jamie's frilly bed. She looked up at him, her eyes filling with unexpected tears.

"I didn't know anything about this," he began.

Lacey turned away from him, looking across the room, taking in the simple details of a five year old's life, hoping to divert the sob that was building in her throat. She stared at Jamie's collection of natural things, her stuffed animals and dolls that filled her toy box to overflowing, the frilly curtains at the window.

Unconsciously, she fingered the wishbone, searching for a way out of the impossible situation.

"Lacey." Jared's voice was velvety soft.

Her heart squeezed in anguish as she reacted to the sound of it. "I shouldn't have come," she whispered as she turned toward him, a hot tear rolling down her cheek.

"Listen to me. I want you to hear me out," he began. "You don't have to say anything, but if *I* don't, I have a feeling I'll always regret it." Jared's voice was tender, almost a murmur.

Lacey nodded, waiting.

"I know you and I have very different beliefs about men and women and how things should be, but I realize that my ideas aren't necessarily always right. At least, I don't think they're right about you."

Lacey blinked, suddenly feeling lightheaded. *What was he saying?*

"I know I'm not what you're looking for, and I know how important your career is to you . . ." His words faded as he closed his eyes.

She watched the play of emotions on his face as he paused. Then he licked his lips, swallowing hard before he continued, his eyes still closed.

"When we were together at the cabin, I can't tell you how different being with you was for me. And if it wasn't special for you, then I need to know."

Jared's eyes opened and she watched as they widened, blazing down into hers. "I fell in love with you that night."

It took several seconds for the words to sink in. *Did she hear him right? He was in love with her?*

"When Jamie gave you that wishbone, I realized how I felt about you. Believe me, I've been fighting it." His smile was tentative. "This is where you can tell me I'm an idiot."

Lacey stared at him, her thoughts whirling uncontrollably. His smile was as intimate as a kiss. She realized the truth in his words: he certainly wasn't what she thought she wanted. He was more.

Jared reached up and cupped her chin, his gaze searching her upturned face. "Children *do* expect their wishes to come true," he whispered, stroking her lower lip with his thumb.

She nodded. Suddenly she wanted to get lost in his eyes, and never look away. There was an eagerness there, an understanding that beckoned to her.

"We're probably . . . obligated to *not* disappoint her." He said the words softly, with quiet emphasis, his hand dropping to take both of hers in his.

As Lacey held his gaze, she slowly began to absorb what he was saying. She licked her dry lips, searching for words. Her mouth wouldn't obey.

"We both could sure use a woman in this house."

Lacey swallowed hard, the lump in her throat threatening this time to break into a joyful sob. Her heart felt like it might explode. Her mind swirled, panicking at the feeling of being out of control.

"I . . . I don't understand what happened." Lacey's words came out in a breathless stammer.

"That makes two of us," Jared's voice was low, almost a whisper. "All I know is that I've been miserable since that weekend with you. I can't sleep at night for thinking about what might have been. I can't explain it away. I don't want to explain it away."

Lacey stared into his eyes, extraordinary, depthless gray eyes. Jamie's father's eyes. Eyes that seemed to be reaching into her thoughts.

As he waited for her response, a vaguely sensuous light passed between them and his gaze became as soft as a caress. He remained quiet, patiently waiting for her reaction.

There was a tingling in the pit of her stomach as Lacey's thoughts swirled and stormed in her mind. There was no doubt he had unlocked her heart and soul, that he had stoked a gently growing fire.

Unexpected happiness filled her as she considered what Jared was suggesting. He did care. He had declared his feelings, the very feelings she'd fought.

"Lacey, I know our worlds might seem incompatible and that you have all sorts of plans and things," he began, "but is there some way we can make it work?"

The idea sent her spirits soaring and she suddenly felt powerless to resist. *Could they? Could there be a way?*

Jared gathered her in a gentle embrace and Lacey buried her face against his neck.

He whispered, his breath hot against her ear, "Would you marry me?"

Lacey pulled away from him to look into his eyes again. *Marry him?* A new and unexpected warmth surged through her as she comprehended what she had heard. Her heart sang with delight as she relaxed, sinking back into his embrace.

Through the roaring chaos of emotions, she breathed one word. "Yes."

EPILOGUE

The staccato sound of hammering ended and the next sound Lacey heard was Jared's voice calling from the roof of the room he was building.

"You ready to go?" he asked.

"Anytime."

For a wedding present Jared had given her blueprints for a customized salon—an addition to their home. The perfect solution to her wants and needs.

She'd happily let the regional job in Denver go, and had insisted Kandy still accept the manager's position. Fairly quickly, though, she found she missed doing hair and especially the interaction with favorite customers.

After much thinking and talking, they'd decided it might be wise for her to take some time off, to get to know the llama business, help Jamie adjust to school, get used to being a mom.

Lacey rubbed her ample belly until the movement there subsided. She had been surprised at how quickly she'd gotten pregnant. Jared claimed it was the mountain air, but she insisted it was because Jamie was in kindergarten half the day and he wouldn't leave her alone.

She smiled, breathing as deeply as her girth allowed.

Jamie bounded into the room and threw her arms around her. She pressed her lips against Lacey's abdomen. "Hello, little sister, how ya doin' in there?"

Lacey rubbed Jamie's back, replying in a squeaky voice, "Doin' fine, but I can't wait to meet you."

Jared walked into the kitchen, jangling his keys. His heart surged at the sight of the two women in his life with their arms wrapped around each other.

"Ladies, the train is leaving. Are you comin' or what?"

As Lacey stared at herself in the salon mirror, a part of her grieved the loss of her waist-length curls. Her mahogany hair now just barely skimmed her shoulders, but she knew it would be much easier to care for when the baby came.

Our baby.

Lacey groaned and rubbed her stomach, shifting in the chair to find a more comfortable position.

"You okay?" Kandy asked as she depressed the foot pedal to lower the hydraulic chair.

"The baby's really pushing. I think she's ready to meet her big sister." She grinned at Kandy's pale, panic-stricken face. "It's not happening right now, silly goose. Relax."

Lacey followed Kandy to the reception area where Jared and Jamie sat waiting. She checked their expressions for approval. Jared flashed an infectious grin.

"Jamie," he said, "look how pretty that lady is. I wonder if she's a movie star."

"Oh, Daddy, that's Mommy." Jamie punched his

arm and he retaliated with a tickle attack until she squirmed out of his reach.

Lacey rolled her eyes. "I don't know them," she said to Kandy.

Jared joined Lacey at the counter. "I'll take care of that, Kandy. What do we owe the manager for this incredible haircut."

"This one's on the house. Consider it a gift for the new baby *and* for the new mom," Kandy said.

Lacey felt Jamie's tiny hand slip into hers and Jared's arm at her not so tiny waist. He gave her a squeeze and she sighed happily. She was really looking forward to a normal waistline. Their lovemaking had modified with her growing form, though Jared's patience and ingenuity had made the entire nine months surprisingly fulfilling and satisfying.

She was the luckiest woman on earth—married to the perfect man, the perfect little angel girl, and a new bundle of joy to add to their perfect little family.

As if he were aware of her thoughts, she felt Jared's mouth touch her ear as he whispered softly, "I love you. Let's go home and get creative."